CLAIMING HER BEASTS
BOOK TWO

DIA COLE

AUTHOR'S NOTE

This is book two in a paranormal/dystopian series based on the rewritten and expanded Heaven in Hell series. Expect a kickass heroine and swoon-worthy beasts who'll have to learn to share.

FYI: This steamy and thrilling ride is not for the faint of heart and some content may be triggering to sensitive readers.

SUMMARY

The city fell. Help never came. Now our lives depend on playing by Dominic's punishing rules. But the icy-cold sergeant's brutal tactics and questionable motives make him just as dangerous as the monsters outside.

Even worse, my visceral attraction to Dominic and a deadly shifter is pushing Reed further into insanity. His bouts of amnesia and animalistic rages may force me to make a soul-shattering choice—love or survival?

❧ I ❧

REED

I woke to find the woman I loved lying naked on top of me. Even more mind-blowing, I was inside her.

Holy shit! I'd give anything to remember how we got to this point. Rubbing my aching head, I glanced around. With the warm water spraying down on us and the lockers running the length of the room around us we had to be in a locker room.

How did we get here?

Lee's wet hair tickled my nose as she nestled her cheek in the hollow of my breastbone. She let out a contented sigh. "I want to stay with you like this forever."

My chest tightened at her words even though I knew it wasn't real. None of this was real. Lee would never cuddle with me, much less have sex with me. Despite us not being related, she still treated me as if I were a younger brother.

I must still be hallucinating. My best friend, Ronnie, had roofied me at my twentieth birthday party last night. I'd been on one hell of a trip ever since then.

First, I'd fantasized that Lee let me go down on her before some ten-foot monster with glowing eyes barged into her room. Then we'd apparently had sex for the first time shortly before our best friends turned into zombies and attacked us. After I'd beat their brains out and acted as the getaway driver for Lee's sister's jailbreak, badass gang members showed up at our house and beat the crap out of me.

And just the other day Ronnie said I lacked creativity. Just wait until I told him about this crazy ass hallucination.

"This isn't a hallucination, cocksucker," a strange voice rumbled in my mind. *"But do us both a favor and go back to sleep."*

Jesus. I'm hearing voices now. Whatever crap Ronnie had given me must have been really strong.

What if I can't wake up from it? My heart pounded.

Ronnie's cousin was once hospitalized for drug-induced psychosis that lasted weeks.

Shit.

"We really should join the others, Not Reed," Lee said, rising over me. Her deep chocolate eyes were slumberous, and her long, hip-length brown hair looked almost black under the spray of the shower.

So captivated by the water running down the slopes of her beautiful breasts it took me a moment to focus on her words. *Why is she calling me Not Reed?*

"She's talking to me," answered the voice in my head.

All at once, the alien presence shoved me to the back recesses of my mind. There I found myself unable to move my body, but still fully aware of everything that was happening to me. Or, more specifically, the things I was doing to Lee.

In one of the most disconcerting moments of my life, I experienced myself leaning up and clamping my lips around one of Lee's nipples.

Her husky moan rang in my ears.

Dazed, I felt my teeth bite down. *Jesus.* That had to hurt.

Lee didn't seem in pain, though. She threw her head back with a wild cry and rocked on my hardening cock.

Whatever controlled my body, gripped her hips and yanked her off my shaft. Then it roughly positioned her on her hands and knees.

"You look so fucking beautiful, dirty dancer," I heard myself say as the entity shoved her thighs apart and knelt behind her on the wet tile.

I couldn't disagree. Lee looked like a goddess with her breasts heaving and her legs splayed. The glistening pink flesh between her toned thighs was the most erotic thing I'd ever seen.

My pierced cock was slowly fed into her.

Jesus. I'd imagined being with Lee all my life, but none of those fantasies came close to this. The sensation of entering her hot, wet pussy was indescribable. Overcome with lust, I forgot about being a bystander and lost myself in the thrill of being inside her.

She moaned and swiveled her hips. "Oh, God. Your barbells, Reed. They're amazing."

I felt a rush of masculine pride. I'd endured the pain of those piercings for her pleasure alone and I'd go through it all again just to hear the music of her husky moans.

"Not Reed," the entity controlling me growled. He grabbed her hair and yanked her head back so fast her teeth snapped together.

"Don't hurt her!" I mentally shouted. But the entity ignored me.

Lee's eyes blazed with fury. "Let go of my hair, *Reed.*"

That's my girl. Lee would let no one, including me, manhandle her.

The entity released her hair, reached around her and pinched her nipple. "What's my name?"

Lee inhaled sharply. "Stop these games, Reed."

"Wrong answer." The entity slipped a hand between her legs and pinched her clit. "What's my name?"

She tried to move away, but my hands gripped her hips forcing her in place.

"Stop hurting her!" I struggled to take control of my body.

"Not Reed," Lee gasped.

"Good." The body snatcher shoved her face to the floor and slammed balls deep inside her. So deep, I swear I could feel her damn cervix.

She let out a broken cry.

The entity hammered into her with deep, savage thrusts.

"Please! Please!" she pleaded over the wet slapping sounds of our bodies.

Lee never begged for anything. I couldn't stand to see the woman I loved so abused.

A rush of white-hot rage gave me the strength to regain control. I immediately jerked myself out of her.

Panting, Lee glanced over her shoulder. "Don't you dare stop."

"Y-you liked that?" I asked, stunned.

"Of course she liked it, cocksucker," that alien voice roared in my mind.

"Go away! Stop talking to me!" I shouted.

Lee twisted all the way around, an expression of outrage on her face.

I held up my hand in an apology. "I didn't mean you, honey. There's someone else talking to me." I tapped the side of my head.

"The name is Hunter."

Lee's irritated look morphed into an expression of concern. "Are you okay?"

"Yes. No. I don't know." I rubbed the painful egg-sized lump on the side of my head. "I don't know what's real and what's not." I had to be hallucinating. But everything felt so real. The pain in my head. The wet spray of the water on my bruised face. The fierce throbbing ache of my cock.

Lee reached up to turn off the shower. As soon as the water cut off, she knelt beside me. "Those gang members really knocked you around."

"But I got some good punches in first, right?" I tried to smile, but only managed to split my lip. The stinging pain added to my growing feeling of discomfort. I hated showing anyone the disfiguring scars on my chest and here I sat naked and exposed in front of her.

"She doesn't care," Hunter interjected. I didn't like that the body snatcher could read my thoughts.

Hunter made a sound of exasperation. *"Of course I can read your thoughts. I'm in your fucking mind."*

"Go away!" I pleaded.

"Reed..." Lee stopped and corrected herself. "Not Reed."

I waved my hand. "Reed is fine."

"Fuck you," groused Hunter.

Lee chewed her bottom lip. "I should have told you earlier that you weren't hallucinating. All of it was real. Ronnie and Cami. The gang members. The apocalypse." She licked her lips. "Us."

I could only shake my head. "No." There was no way. It was too fantastical. Too improbable.

"Listen to her, cocksucker."

Lee looked down at her feet. Like everything else about her, they were perfect. Although I was more of a boob guy, I had to admire how sexy her toenails look painted in that glittery black polish.

"Focus. My mate is talking to you," Hunter snarled.

"Shut up," I muttered back. "She's not your mate."

Lee let out a heavy sigh. "This is my fault. If I'd been straight with you, you never would have charged Javier's men like that. It was suicidal."

I blinked. *Who's Javier?*

"The gang leader. Try to keep up," Hunter admonished.

"Stop it! Just stop talking to me!" I shouted out loud.

Lee reared back.

"You're fucking this up. Let me take over."

I was suddenly hurled into the recesses of my mind. Helpless, I could only observe as Hunter used my body to grab Lee. "So where were we, dirty dancer?"

She pulled away. "Reed, you're scaring me."

"I'm not Reed. Let's finish what we started." Hunter, grabbed my cock and pumped it several times to stiffen it.

Enraged and feeling horribly violated, I mentally shouted, *"Get the fuck out!"* Then I retook control of my body and forced myself to stand. "Lee, stay away from me. There is someone... something inside me. It wants you."

"She's my fucking mate, of course I want her," Hunter shouted. *"She wants me, too."*

"No! She doesn't want you. Leave her alone." My breath came in shallow pants.

Lee's eyes widened, and she stumbled back. "Okay, just calm down." She ran over to a pile of blood-spattered clothes and yanked them on.

"Congratulations, asshole. She's getting dressed."

"Get out of my head!" I slapped my forehead hard enough to make my ears ring.

Hunter went silent for several heartbeats. Just when I thought he'd gone away, he snarled. *"Why don't you get out? I like this body. I'm going to keep it."*

"No, you're not." Turning, I rammed my head against the tile wall. Stars burst across my line of vision and for a blessed moment, that voice quieted.

Lee made a choking sound. "I-I'm going to get you some help."

I hated that I was freaking her out, but I needed her to

leave. "Go," I said, wiping the blood from my nose. "Stay away from me."

In a shocking show of strength, Hunter wrestled control away from me again. "Ignore him. Come back to me, my dirty dancer."

I regained control just in time to stop Hunter from following her out of the room. "No, you don't." Not knowing what else to do, I drove my skull into the closest metal locker.

Bang.

Pain exploded inside my head, along with a wave of dizziness that brought me to my knees. Blood filled my mouth and ran down the back of my throat.

A full minute of silence passed.

Thank Jesus. It worked. Holding my head in my hands, I slowly staggered to my feet.

Hunter chuckled. *"That won't stop me, cocksucker."* Then he took control again.

"Dirty dancer!" I heard myself shout. Helpless, I could only watch as we stumbled out of the locker room and into a gymnasium filled with people.

Dozens of unfamiliar faces gawked at the sight of me. I must have looked like something straight out of a horror movie with my long hair tangled over my bloody face and the scarred mess of my upper body on display.

Most of the women, and several of the men, weren't staring at my face though. They gaped at all the metal running the length of my semi-hard dick.

Fuck no. Being exposed like this in front of so many people was my worst nightmare. But I was helpless to do anything to stop Hunter from plowing through the throngs of people. "Dirty dancer! Get back here!"

A soldier stepped into my path. "Put your clothes on, Hippie."

Holy Shit. The guy looked exactly like my childhood G.I. Joe action figure come to life. Not only did he have biceps bigger than my head, he was equipped with enough weapons to arm a small country.

Hunter didn't seem impressed. "Go fuck yourself, Dom." He tried to shove the man mountain out of our way. When the soldier didn't budge an inch. Hunter balled my hand into a fist and swung at him.

G.I. Joe caught the punch, clenched his powerful hand around mine, and threw my fist back into my face so hard I flew into the air.

People scrambled out of the way as I crashed down. My head slammed against the wood floor with a thwack and everything went dark.

❧ 2 ❧

LEE

Another storm raged outside the Saguaro Valley Christian Academy where we were sheltering. It was the third in so many days. It never normally rained this much in our small desert town. Especially this close to Christmas. Mother Nature must have gotten word about the apocalypse and wanted to come to the party. Or maybe she was grieving for the billions of people who'd lost their lives to the canine flu vaccine that was supposed to save them.

I shuddered, remembering what the vaccine had done to my best friend, Cami. Three days ago, it'd turned her, like most everyone in town, into a cannibalistic monster. No, monster wasn't the right word.

Zombie. Biter. Flesh-eater.

Those were better terms to describe what they had become. They'd died, but somehow their bodies reanimated with the sole purpose of attacking the living. We didn't know if they actually consumed our flesh because they were hungry, or if the Z-virus drove them to attack the living in order to spread the infection. What we knew was that a single bite or scratch from one of them was enough to infect someone. Once infected, there was no hope of survival.

Outside, thunder roared and growled like the ravening creatures gathering in front of the private elementary school. Every day their numbers grew. The soldiers assured us we were protected in here, but then again, they'd also assured us military helicopters would evacuate us days ago.

No one had come to save us. Even worse, rumor had it all communication from the army base had ceased.

We're on our own.

Fear, cold and slippery as a snake, coiled in my stomach. It wasn't for me, though. I was terrified for the only two members of my family left in the world. I'd promised to look after Eden and Reed after Gran died, something I'd managed to do up until now.

Lightning flashed through the desks and chairs barricaded against the windows. The flickering light illuminated the interior of the classroom and the bodies of women and children sleeping around me. Only the pretty, stubborn brunette lying by my side held my focus though.

With her caramel-colored hair, oval face, and cleft chin, Eden was a dead ringer for our mother. At least Gran had always said so. My own memories of Mom and my older sister had grown fuzzy like old, yellowed photographs.

Eden let out a soft snore.

I couldn't help rolling my eyes. The brat could always sleep through anything including Reed's band practices and the loud barking of all the dogs she'd fostered over the years.

Why would a raging storm during the zombie apocalypse be any different?

Shaking my head, I put the long jacket that was serving as my makeshift blanket over her. It'd been cold since the power went out and I didn't want her catching a chill.

The small child burrowed in Eden's arms let out a whimper. I'd forgotten the little girl's name. *Addie? Sofie? Rosie?* Something like that. She'd been separated from her father, who like the other males, was sleeping in one of the other classrooms down the hall.

Always a sucker for lost souls, both the human and animal variety, Eden had taken the curly-haired five-year-old under her wing.

I readjusted the jacket so it covered the sleeping girl too.

A draft of cold air had me rubbing my arms. I was still wearing Reed's blood-splattered shirt, and the feeling of the soft flannel brought his handsome face to mind.

I hope he's okay. A stab of anxiety drew my gaze to the door.

Since knocking him out, Dominic had ordered Reed restrained and kept under observation in the nurse's office.

Worry for him gnawed at me. I didn't like the distance between us. *I'll check on him at dawn.* That was when the soldiers allowed us to leave the classrooms.

Out of habit, I glanced up at the large round clock over the whiteboard at the front of the room. I couldn't make out the placement of the hands, not that it mattered. They'd frozen in place when the power went out.

A bright light flashed in my periphery. I turned to see Zara's pixie-like face lit up by her phone screen. I'd only just met the rainbow-haired, dusky-skinned woman, but her foul-mouth and attitude reminded me so much of Cami, I couldn't help but feel an instantaneous bond with her.

I crawled around the sleeping bodies until I'd made it over to her spot near the windows. "Are you getting a signal?"

"Nah," she whispered back. "The cell towers and the internet are gone." She snorted. "So much for all the fuckers who said it would last months."

"Oh." My heart sank like a stone at the realization we had no communication with the outside world. Not that there was much outside world to communicate with. Saguaro

Valley, like other cities around the world, had fallen the first night of the outbreak. News sites had gone dark along with most social media outlets. A few of our survivor group had been able to reach loved ones on the outside, but that was before the soldiers confiscated all cell phones and communication devices.

"You'd better be careful the soldiers don't find you with that," I warned in a low voice.

Zara rolled a striking pair of hazel eyes at me. "Or what? They'll punish me." She chuckled under her breath. "I'd like some of that action. Especially from that sexy hunk of man-flesh Mike or maybe even Dominic." She made a humming noise and smacked her lips.

The mention of the sergeant in charge made my stomach tighten. The handsome soldier intrigued me more than I wanted to admit. Seeing him knock Reed out in the gym three days ago had definitely cooled off my hormones, though. Reed was lucky Dominic hadn't killed him.

Zara tapped the screen of her phone. "Want to see my boyfriends?"

"Boyfriends? As in more than one?"

"Of course, that monogamy stuff is for suckers. My mom always said to be truly happy, a woman needs a minimum of three lovers entirely devoted to her."

"Really?" I wasn't sure if she was being serious or not.

"This is my harem." She tilted her phone and showed me a photo of three blond, blue-eyed muscular guys with their arms slung around each other.

"Wow." I didn't even try to hide my shock. "So they are okay with you being with all of them?"

"They love it. Most of the time we all get sweaty together if you know what I mean." Her wicked grin reminded me so much of Cami right then, my heart ached.

"Brothers?" I asked, noting the similarities between their blond hair and blue eyes.

"Nah, I just have a type, you know? Do you have a type?"

I shook my head. The three men who'd captured my attention recently couldn't have been more different. Reed would look right at home among Zara's harem with his lanky build, blond hair, and bright blue eyes. Javier, the leader of a dangerous gang, was smaller built and more exotic-looking with his amber eyes and darker skin. And then there was Dominic... My mouth went dry as I thought of the muscular giant.

Forcing the sergeant from my mind, I looked closer at Zara's phone. "Have you heard anything from your boyfriends since..." I trailed off as her smile faded.

"No." She took a deep breath and let it out. "And I don't think I will."

"I'm sorry," I said, not knowing what else to say. We'd all lost people we loved. I still grieved the loss of my Uncle Duncan who'd been killed by Javier's men the morning of the outbreak.

She blinked away the sheen in her eyes and swiped her screen to bring up another photo. It was of her standing with three attractive men who shared her swarthy skin tone and beautiful eyes.

"They're your brothers, right?" I'd seen her eating with them in the cafeteria.

"Yes, and they can be *your* next harem."

Caught off guard, I blinked at her. "What?"

"Dev is the sweet one, and he just turned 18 so he's legal. Sai is a lady's man, but he can be tamed. And Avi is... well he's a prick, but I'm sure you can handle him."

"Mmm-hmm." I pressed my lips together trying not to laugh.

She gave me an expectant look. "So, what do you think?"

"Uh. I'm flattered you'd want to set me up with them, but I'm... kind of with someone already." Just saying that filled me with enough anxiety to make my hands shake. I'd made it my mission to swear off guys, but then I'd gotten drunk and my platonic relationship with Reed had gone up in flames. My skin heated with the memory of how many times we'd had sex in a twenty-four-hour period. It had to be some kind of record.

Zara studied me over the screen of her phone. "Are you talking about Fruitcake?"

I frowned not liking the nickname she'd given him. "Reed's not crazy. He's just been through... a lot." And maybe I was to blame for his condition. I mean, I'd allowed him to think the end of the world was some drug-induced hallucination instead of helping him accept reality.

"No offense, girlfriend. I'm actually a fan of fruitcake. Yum. Nuts and candied fruit. What's not to like?" Zara smacked her lips. "Besides. The crazy ones are always the best in the sack, am I right?"

"You hussies need to be quiet, or else," hissed a heavy, sharp-nosed, middle-aged woman aptly named Karen. When she wasn't complaining to the soldiers about the lack of amenities at the school, she was giving us a hard time.

I mouthed "hussies" to Zara who glared back at the older woman.

"Bring it." Zara yanked a long hunting knife from the inside of her boot and brandished it.

Karen's eyes widened. "I'll report you to the soldiers." She gave me a quick look. "You saw her pull a knife on me."

"Knife? I don't see any knife," I said in a mocking voice. "But I heard you threaten Zara and me. Maybe we should report *that* to the soldiers."

Karen's eyes narrowed. "I see how it is."

"Good, now turn your fat ass around and let me and my

new bestie continue our conversation." Zara twirled her knife in a circle.

Muttering what sounded like obscenities, Karen flopped over with the grace of a beached whale next to her sleeping adult daughter and teenage granddaughter.

"Thanks for having my back," Zara said with a grin.

"Anytime," I replied, watching her slide the knife back into her boot. "You seem pretty sure of yourself with that."

"You should see me with a gun," she said, patting the handgun holstered at her waist. "My mom is Special Forces. She made sure we all learned to shoot before we could ride bikes."

"Sounds as if you're a good person to have around," I joked, mentally cataloging her connection to the military. It seemed she, like everyone else who'd been brought to the school, had a close living relative in the army. My sister and I, on the other hand, didn't.

"Girl, you have no idea. Stick with me and I'll keep you alive. The only thing I want in return is first dibs on the hot soldiers. Deal?" Zara held out her palm.

"Deal," I said, shaking her hand. It felt good to make a friend, even under these circumstances.

My happiness lasted only a moment before the classroom door flew open and a deep voice shouted, "Everyone, on your feet."

$\maltese$　3　$\maltese$

LEE

I exchanged a startled look with Zara as Dominic strode into the room.

"Maybe the chopper is finally here to evacuate us," Zara said over the sudden piercing wail of a toddler. "Or maybe zombies invaded the school."

I gasped, my internal temperature dropping ten degrees.

"Line up by the whiteboard," Dominic ordered, the beam of his flashlight bouncing off the backs of waking people. With his dark close-cropped hair, clean-shaven face, and military fatigues he looked every inch the Special Forces sergeant he was.

I didn't know why but seeing the six-and-a-half-foot tall soldier always took my breath away. It was as if some part of me came alive whenever he was near. Of course, it didn't hurt that his bronze skin, chiseled jaw, and full lips made him one of the most beautiful guys I'd ever seen.

"Look alive, people."

He certainly wasn't the friendliest though. In the three days since we'd been here, I'd only ever seen him bark orders at his soldiers and the other civilians.

"Move it!"

Outside, thunder rumbled as if to underscore the urgency of the order.

Spurred into action, I hurried back to my sister.

Of course, the brat was still sleeping. I roughly shook her awake.

Eden's eyes, the same shade of brown as mine, snapped open. "Wh-what's happening, sissy?"

"Dominic wants us by the white board." Momentarily forgetting about her companion, I yanked my sister's hand to pull her up.

The little girl rolled out of Eden's arms and hit the floor with a panicked shriek.

"Shh, Rosie. It's okay," Eden said, shaking off my hand so she could give the girl a comforting hug. The look she gave me over the girl's shoulder wasn't so comforting.

"Sorry," I mouthed, feeling like an ass. Eden mentioned the girl had witnessed her mother's brutal death. I looked down at the girl's blond curls feeling a stab of sympathy. I too knew the horror of watching my mother die.

"We're just having an early breakfast, right Lee?" My sister gave me a meaningful look.

"Right," I said, playing along. "Maybe we'll have pancakes today." I rubbed my stomach. "Mmm." My acting wouldn't win any awards, but at least it got Rosie to close her mouth and allow Eden to pick her up.

I steered the two of them toward the middle of the line where Zara was holding a spot for us.

"Leave your things here," Dominic shouted at Karen who'd grabbed the oversized wheeled bag she'd brought with her.

The annoying woman gave him a mutinous look and continued rolling her luggage over.

That spurred several other women to run and grab their bags and boxes of personal items.

Must be nice. Other than the clothes on my back and the shoes on my feet, I'd come to the school with nothing. That's not true, I corrected. I had Reed and my sister. *They're the only things that matter.*

I tightened my grip around my sister's elbow. A moment later, we followed a frustrated-looking Dominic out of the classroom.

The battery-operated lanterns strategically placed every four feet on the floor threw eerie shadows on the large hand-print tree mural covering the wall.

"Where are we going?" Eden asked in a hushed voice.

"I don't know," I whispered.

"I'd wager the gym," Zara said, chiming in. "It's the most defensible location in the school."

"Wh-what?" Eden stuttered.

"Well see, you have the hallway that acts as a natural chokepoint and the bleachers that can be climbed for safety. Zombies can't climb, you know?"

Eden and I blinked at her.

Oh, hell. My heart began to pound. "I need to get Reed."

"Relax," Zara said with a dismissive wave. "If zombies were inside the school do you think the soldiers would take their sweet ass time moving us down the hall?"

As if to prove her point, Dominic stopped short and our line bunched together like a compressed accordion.

Ignoring the women stumbling into each other, Dominic motioned at one of his soldiers down the hall. Three days ago, there had been twelve soldiers reporting to him. Now there were only nine.

What happened to the others?

"It's Mike," Eden said in a voice much higher than usual.

She wet her lips, her gaze fixed on the blue-eyed soldier with the blond crew cut.

"Don't tell me you have the hots for Mike," Zara teased.

Eden flushed.

My jaw fell open in surprise. *This is a first.* Up to this point, Eden had rarely shown interest in a guy. I don't know that I entirely approved of her crushing on a soldier, but it wasn't as if he'd return her interest. Dominic had made it clear his squad would not be fraternizing with any of us civilians.

Seeming unaware of Eden's interest, Mike yanked open another classroom door and shouted, "Everyone out."

Slowly, the male members of our group poured into the hallway and fell in step with us. Reunions between family members occurred with hushed whispers and uneasy glances at the soldiers.

"Rosie," a thunderous voice called out.

The little girl twisted around in Eden's arms as a muscular, tattoo-covered man, with a horseshoe mustache, approached them both. "Daddy!"

"We took good care of her, Grady," Eden said as the biker-looking guy yanked Rosie away.

"My daughter should stay with me," he grunted, holding the child against the front of his sleeveless denim jacket. "They're assholes for separating parents from their children." He sneered at the soldiers and carried Rosie to the back of the line.

Eden sighed. "He does have a point."

"His point reeks of alcohol." I fanned the air to dissipate the smell of vodka. The little girl was probably better off with my sister than that drunk.

Zara tapped her chin thoughtfully. "We need to find out where Grady is keeping his stash."

"What stash?" asked a handsome, dusky-skinned man who'd appeared behind her. "Are you holding out on me, sis?"

"No, Sai."

"Are you sure?" He rubbed his knuckles against the top of Zara's rainbow hair. With his mop of curls, hazel eyes, and rakish goatee, I could see how this brother would be the lady killer.

Zara elbowed him in the stomach. "Don't embarrass me in front of my new friends."

Sai's hazel eyes skipped over my sister and crashed into me. He gasped audibly and put one ring-covered hand over his heart. "Have I died?"

Zara rolled her eyes. "No, but right now I wish you would."

Sai stepped around her. "Then how do you explain this angel?" As he approached, I got an eyeful of the gold chains hanging around his neck. They were impossible to miss with his black silk shirt unbuttoned clear to his rock-hard abs. Out of habit, I glanced down at his shoes. Cami always said you could tell a lot about a guy from his shoes.

Sai's leather Gucci loafers put him in the big spender category. If we were in the club, I'd be bleeding his wallet dry with lap dances and trips to the VIP room. Based on the gleam in his eye, he'd have taken the bait hook, line and sinker.

"I'm Sai Sighn," he said, taking my hand. "And I'd sing for you, darling." He smiled, flashing me a pair of dimples that made me swoon a little.

He looked somewhat familiar. Maybe I'd seen him at the club.

Zara shoved him hard in the back. "Her name is Lee and she already has a boyfriend."

Sai didn't budge and his smile never wavered. "Maybe she could use another." As he kissed the top of my knuckles, I caught a whiff of his bay rum cologne.

It brought back the memory of my last night at the club.

Javier, also a flamboyant dresser and a wearer of expensive cologne, had summoned me to his table to proposition me. Then he'd sent his men to my house where they'd attacked Reed and killed my uncle. Feeling suddenly sick to my stomach, I snatched my hand from Sai's.

Sai's eyes widened in surprise.

"Looks as if your charm has run out, brother," called out a taller, more muscular version of Sai. The new guy, who was rocking the shaved head look, had to be Avi.

I studied Zara's eldest brother as he prowled over in a black T-shirt, jeans, and combat boots. His rough-hewn features included a heavy brow, a stubbled jaw, and a nose that looked as if it had been broken more than once. He was definitely more rugged looking than handsome. Even so, there was something wild and predatory in his gold-green eyes that heated my blood.

"Sai's going down in flames," chortled an acne covered teenage guy in glasses who sidled up next to Zara.

Zara high-fived him. "Nice one, Dev." Her smile faded as she caught Avi's censured gaze. "Hey, Avi."

Avi frowned and raked his gaze over me in a way that made me feel lacking. "Who is this? And why are you wasting time talking to her?"

What an asshole.

"These are Zara's new friends." Sai motioned at me. "Avi and Dev meet Lee and..." He turned to Eden and seemed to draw a blank.

Eden pursed her lips. "I'm Eden, Lee's less attractive younger sister."

I winced. "That's not true." Eden was pretty in the same girl-next-door kind of way my mother had been. I on the other hand, had more exotic features like my father. They and my huge breasts seemed to attract more male attention.

"I agree," Dev said, giving Eden a shy smile.

Avi made an impatient sound. "Enough pleasantries, where is your go-bag, Zara? You know better than to be without it."

Zara rolled her eyes. "Whatever. Sai doesn't have his."

"That's because all he packed were boxes of condoms," Dev said with a snort.

Sai winked at me. "It's all about priorities."

Avi's narrowed gaze bounced between Sai and Zara. "Mom would be so disappointed in you two."

I didn't like the stricken expression on my new friend's face. Wanting to help her out, I said, "The sergeant instructed us to leave our things in the classroom."

"Really?" Avi stared down the hallway where Dominic and Mike were speaking in low voices. "We're not evacuating then?"

"Or they don't want to overload the helicopter," Eden said, her gaze locking on Mike again.

Up ahead, Mike nodded at whatever Dominic had told him. "Yes, sir," he said audibly, before approaching the people at the front of our line. "Everyone, please follow me into the gym. Once inside, find a seat on the bleachers."

His announcement was met with loud murmurs. A few people shouted out questions.

"Are we being evacuated?"

"Are the helicopters here?"

I tensed, wondering if I should find Reed. The nurse's office was clear on the other side of the school near the chapel.

"Silence," Dominic shouted, his deep voice reverberating in the narrow hallway.

Everyone went quiet and still. Even the wailing toddler stopped crying.

"Follow Mike," Dominic snarled.

Immediately people moved toward the gym.

I sucked in a breath as I passed the imposing sergeant. For a fleeting moment, Dominic's black gaze tangled with mine and my heart skipped a beat. Once again, I felt that strange magnetism between us. It filled me with the ridiculous urge to throw myself into his arms. Thankfully, I was able to force my gaze to the back of Zara's rainbow-hued curls.

Eden leaned over and whispered, "If this is an evacuation, they better bring the animals too." She motioned in the direction of the library where the survivors' pets were being kept. My sister had been helping take care of the animals, mainly cats, the other survivors had refused to leave behind.

I rolled my eyes. For some inane reason, my sister equated the lives of animals with human lives. Her veganism was understandable, but her previous arrests for protesting the canine euthanization laws were not. Trying to keep my sarcastic remarks to myself, I focused on following the line into the gym.

Someone had turned on a portable floodlight by the stage in the back. The light was so garishly bright I had to look down at the shiny wood floor so my eyes could adjust. Even though our group had spent a good deal of time in this space over the past few days, it still smelled faintly of floor wax and buttered popcorn.

"Look, Reed is here," Eden said, tugging my arm.

My heart jumped. I quickly scanned the bleachers until I found him seated in the third row from the top. He was turned away from us and most of his face was obscured by the sweatshirt hood he'd drawn over his head, but I'd know his lanky build anywhere.

"Reed!" I called out, frustrated when he didn't look in our direction. *Damn.* There were too many people in my way. I chewed my bottom lip, as the line crawled along at a snail's pace. It seemed to take forever for us to climb the mostly filled bleachers.

Zara went up two rows and sat. "Lee, over here."

I shook my head and motioned at the top of the bleachers. "I'm sitting up there."

Zara's brothers had followed their sister into the second row, but she shoved past them to step back into the aisle.

Several people behind us grumbled.

"Zara, sit down," exclaimed Avi.

"You stay. I don't want to sit with you anyway." Turning her back on her brothers, Zara followed Eden and me up the bleachers.

As we climbed higher, I dropped my sister's arm and took the steps two at a time. When I reached Reed's nearly empty row, I ran over to him. "Reed!" I sat down and threw my arms around his neck. Never had I been happier to inhale his earthy clove scent.

When he didn't return my embrace, I slowly pulled away. "Reed?"

He didn't look at me.

What's going on? Is he mad at me? Confused, I gently turned his bearded face toward mine.

He stared at me with no recognition.

My stomach dropped. *What happened to him?*

Eden, who'd sat on the bench next to me, gasped. I didn't know if she was shocked by the bruised massacre of his normally model-gorgeous face or the dullness in his unblinking electric blue eyes.

"Is Fruitcake okay?" Zara asked in a loud voice.

Kiara, a heavily pregnant woman, sitting a few rows down, spun around. "The nurse gave him and Vincent enough meds to tranq elephants."

Her boyfriend, Mario, a dark-haired man whose arms and

neck were covered in gang tattoos, laughed. "*Cabron* is flying high. I want some of that shit."

Kiara smacked the back of her boyfriend's head.

My anxiety grew as I studied Reed's expressionless face.

Vincent, a reed-thin man with a weather-beaten face and wild eyes, muttered nonsense on the same bench several feet away. The sour smell coming off the formerly homeless guy made my eyes water and his strange chanting made the hair on the back of my neck rise.

"Why did you choose the looney tunes section?" Sai groused as he sat down next to Zara. It seemed he and his brothers had followed us up after all.

"Lee wanted to sit next to Fruitcake." Zara lowered her voice slightly. "You know, the crazy guy."

Dev, who was sliding into the same row, glanced between Reed and Vincent. "Which crazy guy?"

"Reed isn't crazy," Eden snapped.

Dev flushed and stammered an apology.

Avi found a seat in the top row and made a sound of annoyance. "Sit down and be quiet."

Zara spun around to glare at him. "Stop treating us like children."

"I will when you stop acting like children," he shot back.

"Go fuck your—" Zara broke off at the sound of the gym door being kicked open.

❧ 4 ❧

DOMINIC

s I stood in the gymnasium doorway, I tightened my grip around the remains of Dr. Bloom.

The former dentist thrashed against me, but I easily held him in place. He gnashed his teeth, but the leather jacket tied around his head kept him from biting anyone. *More's the pity.* I had half a mind to throw the infected man at those entitled civilians and walk away from this mess. But that would go against orders.

A good soldier always follows orders.

Dr. Bloom's widow let out a broken sob behind me. Her grief didn't absolve her and her husband of their actions. Because of them, one of my soldiers was dead.

Rage flickered inside me, hot and bright. Only decades of conditioning kept me from losing control of my temper. "Follow me," I ordered through clenched teeth.

Gasping for breath, the hyperventilating blond woman nodded.

To ensure her compliance, I shackled her elbow with my free hand while still keeping hold of her husband's zip-tied arms. Then I dragged the Blooms to the center of the basket-ball court.

I stood and waited for the gasps and murmuring of the civilians in the bleachers to cease. After a minute, I lost my patience and shouted, "Quiet," in my drill sergeant voice. It'd been effective in commanding the attention of thousands of soldiers over the years and it did not fail me now.

The sudden hush that settled over the room was gratifying. Clearing my throat, I glared at the pitifully weak civilians the colonel had charged me and my soldiers with protecting. Without our intervention they would already be dead.

Maybe they should be.

I spied a stunningly beautiful face near the top of the bleachers and immediately retracted that thought. *She's among them.* The female that had fascinated me since I'd encountered her standing over a pile of corpses, smoking gun in hand.

Lee.

No female had ever captured my interest the way she had. Now I was compelled by some primal instinct to ensure her survival. Something that would be a hell of a lot easier if she and the rest of these civilians would follow my rules.

Grimacing, I roughly thrust Danika out in front of me. "You all know Danika Bloom."

The blond sprawled out on the floor.

Raising my voice, I said, "Yesterday, Danika and her husband snuck out of the school. At zero hundred hours, they attempted re-entry by ramming a sports utility vehicle through the front gates." The idiots actually took a portion of the wrought-iron gate down before being surrounded by a horde of infected.

The civilians met my announcement with gasps and wide-eyed gazes.

"My soldiers saved Danika and re-secured the gate, but it cost Private Alaggio his life." The human soldier had barely been out of bootcamp. Even so, he'd fought against the infected bravely and courageously. His life was worth dozens of that bitch on the floor. Anger smoldered inside me as I scowled at the sobbing woman.

"Dr. Bloom was also killed during the incident." With a flare of showmanship, I ripped off the leather jacket covering the former dentist's head.

The sight of his half-chewed off face caused the expected uproar among the civilians.

"He's a zombie!"

"It's a Biter!"

"He'll attack us!"

I allowed their terror to build, even pushing Dr. Bloom closer to the first row.

Collective cries rang out as the civilians shrank back.

Mike, who watched from the base of the bleachers, gave me a sharp look.

I didn't need his warning. The many wars we'd served in had shown me how destructive human panic and fear could be. But fear could also be harnessed.

Dr. Bloom thrashed and twisted his head around trying to bite me. With his eyes rolling white and bloody saliva frothing from his lips, the infected man looked and acted like a rabid beast. And much like a rabid beast, he needed to be put down.

In a quick motion born of decades of training, I unsheathed a dagger from my tactical vest and stabbed him through the back of his head. Then I jerked it out of his skull, wiped the blade clean on his blue windbreaker, and dropped the former dentist's corpse next to his wife.

Danika scurried away from her husband's lifeless body and

let out an ear-splitting wail. "W-we just wanted to get Kona. He's like our child.... He was like our child." She sobbed harder likely because the terrier had been mortally injured by the same zombies that had killed her husband. "It's your fault, Sergeant Rosario. You should have just let us bring him here."

Her sad attempt at justifying her actions only inflamed my fury. "Dogs are carriers of the canine flu. In attempting to bring the animal here, you put the lives of every man, woman, and child here at risk." I motioned at the people in the bleachers.

Danika wilted under the scorn in my voice and the icy glares from the other civilians. It was obvious she either hadn't considered the ramifications of her actions, or she really didn't give a damn about anything other than her potentially virus-spreading animal.

She wasn't alone in her selfish mentality. I turned my scowl on the civilians in the bleachers. None of them had offered to assist my squad in fortifying and defending the school. That would change immediately.

I cleared my throat. "None of you will survive on your own. However, if you wish to leave, now is your chance."

The civilians exchanged confused glances.

I stepped around Danika and addressed the crowd. "I'm offering everyone in this room the opportunity to leave right now. No questions asked." I glanced behind me. "Sergeant Williams, please open the back door."

Mike gave me an incredulous look but strode over to the door to the right of the stage. As he opened it, a gust of wind blew in carrying the musty scent of ozone. Outside, torrential rain poured from the dark sky, while lightning strobed the wide-open field.

I motioned at the door. "You are free to go." I was bluffing. I'd never let them leave. But years ago, when I was training to be a handler, the colonel taught me an important lesson.

Force them, and they'll resist. Let them think they have a choice, and they'll commit.

"But what about the military evacuation?" A burly man in his mid-forties blurted out.

I gave the man an assessing look, my gaze drawn to the leatherneck tattoo on his beefy forearm.

I can use a former marine.

Clearing my throat, I said, "Those that stay will be evacuated."

"When will that be?" shouted a younger, taller, pock-marked version of the first man. He wore a T-shirt that read, 'Semper Fi.'

Two former marines. Even better.

"I don't know," I admitted. "Maybe tomorrow. Maybe three months from now. But the helicopters will come." The colonel wouldn't have prioritized the rescue of these civilians only to abandon them.

I let the civilians chew on that for a few moments then added, "You all are free to choose, but you are not free from the consequences of your choice. Those that leave won't be permitted to return. Those that stay must follow my rules and pull their weight. There will be no freeloaders."

One of the toddlers let out a well-timed cry.

"Children and the infirm are exempt," I added.

A few civilians smiled.

A Hispanic man sitting near the top of the bleachers stood. "What if I want to go, but my girlfriend wants to stay?" He pointed at the pregnant woman sitting next to him.

The woman let out an outraged cry.

I re-sheathed my knife and extracted a piece of paper

from my pocket. It contained the names of everyone I'd been instructed to protect along with notes on those who'd been rescued with them. "You're Mario Hernandez, correct?"

He nodded.

"My notes show your girlfriend was not on the initial save-list. Therefore, if you leave, her invitation to stay is revoked. She will need to leave with you." Supplies were limited. We couldn't waste them on non-essential civilians.

A wave of murmurs ran through the crowd.

Deciding to make their choice simpler, I carefully unfolded the entire list. "When I call your name, please stand."

Over the next few minutes, I read the names on the initial list. When I got to the end, roughly half of the civilians were standing, including Danika.

After giving the woman a glare, I walked the length of the bleachers, memorizing the faces of those I'd been ordered to save. None of the elderly or children were among them. But Lee was there, standing beside her sister.

Before her beautiful face could distract me, I forced my attention to the rest of the civilians. "If you're seated, under-stand that you owe your place here to the family member or friend on the save-list. If that person leaves, you must leave with them. If they violate my rules and are exiled, you'll be exiled with them."

Family members exchanged anxious glances.

I clapped my hands together loudly. "Now, sit down and decide if you will stay or go. You have three minutes."

Up in the bleachers, Lee rubbed the back of the hooded man seated next to her. I tensed, trying to place him.

It's the hippie-looking guy who caused all the commotion the first day. Who is he to her?

When I'd rescued them, she'd called him her roommate.

But she's not holding him like he's her roommate. She's holding him like he's her lover.

An unfamiliar emotion made me grind my teeth together. It couldn't be jealousy though. One had to care for someone to be jealous. And I cared for no one other than my beast. Attachments made soldiers weak.

A weak soldier is a dead soldier.

Needing to focus on something other than my unsettling reaction to Lee, I turned my gaze to the intriguing group of civilians seated next to her. I could tell by their coloring they were Prisha's children. If they had even a fraction of the legendary Titan's strength and training, they'd be a formidable fighting force. Particularly the Lykos.

I made a low noise of approval as I studied Avi Sighn. His wolf-shifting abilities were currently suppressed, but once unleashed, he'd make for a powerful beast.

A beast that will need a handler.

Unfortunately, I was the only trained handler here and I'd already re-paired myself to Hunter. Hoping for a change in my beast's status, I glanced down at the biometric scanner grafted to my forearm. Hunter's blood oxygen and heart rate were normal, but he still had no brain activity. Even more disturbing, when I reached for him through our beast-handler bond, I found only emptiness.

What happened to him?

"Everyone, listen to me," Danika called out loudly, shaking me from my thoughts. "Don't leave the school. Those things... those monsters are everywhere."

Having had quite enough of the woman, I waved her away. "Leave now."

Danika's tear-stricken face went bone-white. "What? No."

"You endangered the civilians and got my soldier killed. Leave."

"B-but I'm on the save-list," she sputtered.

"Not anymore." I'd put a line through her name.

"Nooo!" she howled. "I'll die out there."

"Your other option is to die here." I tapped my holstered handgun.

A shocked silence descended on the room.

I wasn't bluffing now. She'd be an example for the others.

"You can't let him do this!" Danika looked out into the bleachers as if searching for someone to come to her defense.

Lee's younger sister stood, her expression a mixture of concern and outrage.

Lee jumped up next to Eden, slapped her hand over her sister's mouth, and dragged her back into her seat.

I mentally applauded the dark-haired female who made me want things I couldn't have. Then I turned back to Danika. "I will not ask you again. Leave."

Seeming to shrink in on herself, Danika stumbled around her dead husband and walked to the door.

Mike grabbed her arm and thrust her outside. He'd escort her to the front gate. Danika would be dead by morning. But she had no one to blame but herself.

There are consequences for insurrection.

I should know. I'd been serving a life sentence for defying my orders before the colonel reinstated me three days ago.

Turning my attention to the rest of the civilians, I said, "Who wants to join Danika?"

Unsurprisingly, no one came forward.

I nodded, pleased they were showing common sense. "You've made a wise choice."

"Ready, Sarge?" a husky voice called out.

I glanced over at the dark-skinned female soldier who stood in the gymnasium doorway. "Yes, thank you, Corporal Ross."

Motioning in Darcy's direction, I said, "Before returning to your assigned quarters, you will meet with Corporal Ross to receive your assignments. Every able-bodied person over the age of sixteen will receive a team and a group assignment. Everyone, regardless of age, will be expected to follow the safe house rules and my rules for survival."

"What are the rules?" the Lykos called out.

Ah. I liked him better and better. "Excellent question."

LEE

"Ugh. Why did we have to sit in the top row of the bleachers?" complained Sai through a mouthful of sunflower seeds. "It'll take us at least another half an hour to get out of here." The handsome man waved at the line of people waiting to speak to Darcy.

I gave him an apologetic smile as I rested my head against Reed's shoulder. It sucked that we'd be the last ones out of the gym, but on the plus side, Kiara and her boyfriend had moved several rows down, so we had most of this section of the bleachers to ourselves now. With the rain beating against the large square windows behind our heads, it was almost relaxing.

Besides, I wanted to spend more time with Reed before being separated from him again.

Letting out a deep sigh, Sai looked between me and Reed. Then he lolled his head back on the legs of his sleeping older brother. "It just adds insult to injury."

I wasn't sure if he was talking about our situation or me being with Reed.

Dev looked at Sai from over the thick rims of his glasses. "We can deal you into the next game."

"Yeah, you'd be more of a challenge," Zara announced, throwing down her cards in front of Dev. "Ah ha! Royal flush, you lose. Pony up your seeds."

Dev groaned and pushed some of his sunflower seeds at Zara.

"Be glad we're not playing for bullets," Zara chortled as Dev gathered the cards and shuffled them.

The siblings' camaraderie had me thinking of Eden and wondering where she was. She'd stormed down the steps of the bleachers as soon as Dominic finished his lecture and had gotten the first assignment from Darcy.

I knew Eden was furious at me because I'd stopped her from trying to intervene with Danika. But I didn't want her getting exiled from the school along with the stupid dentist's wife.

I couldn't believe Danika would try to bring a dog here. And taking out the front gate—the only barrier between us and the monsters—was unforgivable.

Eden would get over her anger with me. She always did. In the meantime, it didn't hurt to give her a little space. Especially since I knew she couldn't go anywhere.

After the Blooms' actions, Dominic's squad would have the school locked down tighter than Reed's bongo drums.

"I'm just glad Avi had playing cards and snacks in his backpack," Dev said, motioning at his eldest brother who lay on the top row behind us.

Zara scoffed. "Avi is always prepared for everything. Even the apocalypse." She glanced at me. "Lee, you want in this round?"

"No, thanks," I said, rubbing my face against the soft fabric of Reed's sweatshirt. Inhaling his earthy clove scent was soothing and I could really use the calm. It'd been hours since we'd been paraded into the gym and asked to choose between staying and leaving. After having heard Dominic's exhaustive list of rules, I'd been left wondering if we'd made the right choice by staying.

The sergeant was essentially demanding we trade our freedom for his protection. In return for staying at the school, he'd control every waking moment of our lives including what and when we ate, and even when we slept.

As someone who'd been on their own since eighteen, I found the idea troubling. *But it might be the only way to keep Eden and Reed safe.*

I squeezed Reed's arm, hoping he'd wake up. "Come back to me, honey."

Vincent who'd nodded off a few feet away woke with a start. "The Queen is coming. We honor and worship her immortal glory in this realm and all others. May she bless her disciples with her undying power and righteous rule, and may the Kingdom of the Kindred be without end. Amen."

He chanted his weird prayer over and over, his voice getting louder.

Zara, Dev, and Sai stared at the raving man.

Mario spun around in his seat several rows down. "Hey *loco*, shut the fuck up."

Vincent acted as if Mario had called him over. He climbed down to where Mario sat with Kiara. "You're a disciple too, pray with me."

Mario raised one of his tattooed fists. "I'll give you something to pray about."

"Not here, *papi*." Kiara dragged her boyfriend down the bleachers while Vincent followed after them.

I guess I should feel grateful Reed wasn't that far gone. *Or is he?* Sighing, I rested my face against his shoulder.

"Lee?" Reed said, in a voice so faint, I wondered if I'd imagined it. He slowly turned his head to look at me.

Relieved to see recognition in his gorgeous blue eyes, I hugged him as hard as I could.

"Ouch," he said, pulling back. One cut near his lip opened and bled.

"Sorry," I said, reminding myself to be gentle with him. "I'm just so glad you're... yourself. You scared me there for a while."

"You were acting like a zombie," Zara said, glancing at Reed over her cards. She caught herself and winced. "Sorry, bad choice of words."

"No need to apologize." Reed rubbed his head. "The drugs make me really out of it, but they stop him from talking to me."

Zara frowned and exchanged uneasy looks with Dev and Sai.

My stomach sank. I'd hoped that Reed's episode in the locker room had been a one-time thing. Lowering my voice, I said, "Are you still hearing the voices in your head?"

"There's only one voice." Reed blotted his bloody lip with the cuff of his sweatshirt. "And no, I'm not hearing Hunter right now, thank Jesus."

Hunter? I didn't think naming imaginary voices was a good sign, but I focused on the fact that Reed seemed back to normal. Leaning over, I rubbed his leg. "I missed you."

Reed drew me into his arms. "I missed you too."

My head fit perfectly under his chin. As I listened to his heart thudding against my ear, a lot of the tension I'd been carrying evaporated.

"What a crazy few days, eh? Who would have thought we'd ever be in a real zombie apocalypse?" Reed kissed the top of my head. "How are you holding up?"

It was the simplest of questions and it should have been the easiest thing in the world to lie and tell Reed I was fine. But a softball lodged in my throat and my eyes watered.

Things were not fine. Uncle Duncan was dead. The city had fallen, and Dominic had all but admitted we weren't getting evacuated any time soon. I felt my face crumble before a sob escaped my lips.

Reed dragged me into his lap and gave me one of those bear hugs I'd missed so badly. "It's okay, honey. You don't always have to be the strong one."

But I did. For his sake. For Eden's sake. It was the way it had always been, and it was the way it'd always be. Taking a shuddering breath, I wiped my eyes. "I'm okay. We're all going to be okay."

"Maybe we'd be better off if we left this place though. I don't trust G.I. Joe," Reed nodded down at Dominic.

The dark-haired sergeant stood at the bottom of the bleachers glaring directly at us. The menace in Dominic's black eyes curdled my stomach. He looked as if he wanted to kill something, possibly us.

"I don't trust him either," I said, forcing my gaze from the man. Despite the strange way Dominic made me feel, or maybe because of it, I sensed he was a threat. The emotionless way he'd knifed Dr. Bloom and then kicked the dentist's wife out of the school had been chilling.

I took a deep breath and let it out. "On the other hand, I think he and his soldiers may be our best chance of survival... for now."

Reed nodded slowly as we touched our foreheads together. "Then we stay... for now."

"For now," I echoed.

He brushed his nose against mine.

This new intimacy between us felt strange, but good. Really good. I snuggled closer wondering how he still managed to look sexy. "How can you look so hot with a black eye?" I blurted out.

His lips curved up. "You're looking hot, too." He tapped

the top button of the flannel shirt I was wearing. "You look good wearing my clothes."

The devil made me say, "I look better wearing no clothes."

Reed inhaled sharply, and I felt his muscles and other parts of his body tighten.

Memories of what we'd been doing in the locker room before he'd gone psycho made my skin heat. Even though I had no conscious thought of kissing him, suddenly my lips were pressed against his.

"Lee," he groaned, his tongue sweeping into my mouth.

I invited him in, sucking on his tongue while I rocked against him. Heat pulsed low in my body and my breasts ached for his touch.

As if reading my mind, he caressed my nipple through my shirt.

I moaned, sliding my hand under his sweatshirt. He wore nothing underneath and his skin warmed my fingers.

"Damn, this is better than any movie," Zara said, bursting my romantic bubble.

Sai made a sound of agreement. "Especially if it turns X-rated."

Ah hell. For a moment, I'd forgotten we weren't alone. Taking a ragged breath, I broke away from Reed.

Sai, Dev, and Zara were staring at us with way too much interest.

"Please continue," Sai said, kicking his expensive loafers up on the bench in front of him. "Dev needs some sex education."

The teenager's face turned beet red. "I do not."

Sai snorted. "You've been raised by this thirty-year-old virgin." He tapped his older brother's leg. "Of course, you do."

"Who are they?" Reed whispered in my ear.

"The Sighn family," I whispered back.

Zara giggled. "You're not being fair, Sai. I'm sure Avi told Dev all about the birds and the bees, or at least showed him some good porn sites, right?" She gave Dev a pointed look.

The poor guy looked as if he wanted the bleachers to swallow him whole. "We're not having this conversation."

Sai leaned forward and clapped him on his back. "There's nothing to be ashamed of. I was inexperienced when I was your age too."

Zara rolled her eyes. "When you were his age, you'd signed your first multi-million-dollar contract and had been with more women than currently occupy this zip code."

Sai pursed his lips. "Don't be ridiculous."

"I'm not counting the dead ones," Zara retorted.

"Ah, you may be right," Sai looked over his sister's head to give me a sheepish grin. "In my defense, I've been searching for my perfect women. Maybe you're one of them, Lee."

Reed jerked upright and twisted around to look at Sai.

Oh, crap. This could be bad. The old Reed rarely lost his temper. But I didn't know how this unstable version would respond to another guy blatantly hitting on me.

Reed practically shoved me out of his lap and scrambled into Sai's row.

"Reed!" I called out, trying to grab him before he attacked Sai.

But Reed only sat down next to him. "You're Sai Sighn. The Sai Sighn."

"The one and only." Sai gave a theatrical half-bow.

Reed's expression turned to amazement. "Lee, this is the lead singer of the Cocktail Kings." He grabbed Sai's hand and shook it wildly.

Sai gave him a dazzling smile, clearly enjoying the reaction. "I take it you're a fan."

Reed sputtered. "Jesus. Yes. I have all your albums. Lee likes your music too." At my blank look he said,

"Remember he's the guy that won America's Top Singer years ago?"

I didn't, but I nodded anyway.

Reed stared at Sai with a look of wonder. "My friend Ronnie and I were going to drive to Vegas to see your show before all the canine flu crap happened."

Sai's smile dimmed. "The canine flu ruined a lot of things."

Reed, still holding Sai's hand, continued staring at him. "What's a super star like you doing in Saguaro Valley?"

Sai dragged his hand away. "I was visiting family for Christmas." He gave Zara and Dev affectionate looks.

"And we're so glad you did," Zara said, smacking him on his leg. "Can you imagine if you hadn't taken me up on my invitation?"

Sai stroked his goatee. "Hmm. Instead of sitting in a crowded gym being threatened by soldiers, I'd be in my LA mansion with my supermodels."

"Your supermodels?" I repeated with a laugh.

"He dates a flock of them at a time," Zara said rolling her eyes. "They're all skanky hos."

"They are not," Sai said with mock offense. "And, I have to admit, I'd much rather ride out the apocalypse with them than you."

Zara flicked a sunflower seed at him.

Sai ducked, and the seed landed on Avi's face.

Avi bolted upright, blinking his eyes. "Is it our turn?"

"Actually, it looks like it," Dev said, motioning down at the few remaining people waiting for Darcy.

"Good," Avi said, brushing off his jeans. He noticed Reed sitting next to Sai and his eyes narrowed. "The sooner we leave the company of these lunatics, the better."

"Avi!" Zara said, sounding shocked and annoyed. "That's rude, even for you."

I glared at the big guy wondering how I ever thought he was attractive.

"No worries," Reed said with one of those easy grins that squeezed my heart. He turned to Sai. "You've got to jam with me sometime, man."

Sai gave him a dimpled smile. "Oh, are you a musician?"

Reed nodded. "I'm a bassist, but I also know my way around a guitar and keyboard."

"He's self-taught," I added. Although I'd never encouraged Reed's musician dreams, I'd always been proud of his natural talent. He was amazing at everything he did. From baseball to music, to making love.

My breath grew choppy and for a moment I fantasized about dragging Reed somewhere private to finish what we'd started earlier.

Avi sniffed the air and gave me an intense look that made me shiver.

Sai grinned at Reed. "Sure. Why not? There has to be a music room in this school. Let's find ourselves some instruments and see what you've got."

"There won't be time for that," Dominic said in a clipped tone.

All six of us jumped at the sight of the massive soldier staring up at us from three rows down.

Crap! Where did he come from? The sergeant definitely hadn't been there a moment ago. *How the hell could he have climbed the bleachers so fast without us seeing him?*

Avi was the only one who didn't seem taken aback. He stood and straightened his shoulders. "Is it time for our assignments, sir?"

Dominic seemed to thaw a bit at Avi's respectful tone. "Yes, please speak with Corporal Ross."

We all stood, not needing further prompting.

Reed swayed as if the quick movement was a little disorienting for him.

Sai reached out to steady him, an action that made me like the rock star even more.

Reed gave him a grateful look as Zara gathered the playing cards and snacks to give back to her oldest brother.

Dominic intercepted the handoff. "Safe house rule number five, no unauthorized consumption of food." He snatched the bag of sunflower seeds from her grasp.

Zara glared at him. "What the hell?"

Avi pushed her aside. "We're sorry, sir. It won't happen again."

"See that it doesn't," Dominic warned.

Zara looked as if she wanted to spit glass, but she allowed Avi to steer her into the aisle and follow Dev down to the gym floor.

Sai descended after his siblings with Reed on his heels.

It seemed my lover had all but forgotten about me. Wondering if I should be jealous of Reed's obvious man-crush on Sai, I moved into the aisle.

Dominic stepped in front of me. "I need to speak with you, Ms. Walker."

❧ 6 ❧

LEE

As I stood in the aisle of the bleachers two rows above Dominic, I realized I was in trouble.

Big trouble if the ticking muscle in the sergeant's jaw was any indication.

"Did I do something wrong?" I couldn't have broken one of his rules already.

"The show you and Hippie put on a few minutes ago was inappropriate." Dominic's tone practically frosted the air around us.

"Hippie?" I said in confusion.

"Him," Dominic sneered, jabbing his thumb at Reed's back.

Reed and the Sighns had almost reached the basketball court without noticing I was still waylaid at the top.

"I'm not sure what you're talking about." I refused to let Dominic embarrass me. It wasn't as if I'd given Reed a lap dance or we'd taken our clothes off or anything. I had nothing to be ashamed about and the sergeant was an ass to call me out on it. "Now if you'll excuse me. I want to catch up to my friends." I motioned for Dominic to step out of my way.

Moving too fast for me to track, the sergeant raced up the steps and grabbed my arm. "You're not excused."

The dizzying speed in which he moved brought to mind another muscular soldier. He'd grabbed me too.

The gym vanished, and I was suddenly back in my childhood bedroom fighting a monster.

He picks me up by my throat.

"Daddy," I manage to choke through his clenched fingers.

The blank look in his eyes terrifies me.

I struggle to breathe. "Daddy, please."

He lifts the knife—

"Ms. Walker," Dominic said loudly, his voice tearing me from the nightmare.

All at once the sergeant's handsome face and the gym blinked back into focus.

My breath came in shallow pants as I tried to calm myself.

The past can't hurt me.

I closed my eyes and tried to stop the tremors wracking my body.

The past can't hurt me.

I focused on the rain pattering against the windows behind me. The soothing rhythm calmed me down enough that I could suck in some air.

"Are you okay, Ms. Walker?" Dominic's voice was gentle, almost sympathetic.

I didn't want his sympathy.

Snapping my eyes open, I glared at him. Although logically I knew it wasn't Dominic's fault he triggered a flashback, I blamed him just the same. "Don't touch me."

The sergeant released my arm and backed down two steps. "Tell me what happened just now."

No. I didn't have to tell him anything. I was so sick of his imperious attitude. First, he dragged us all here in the middle of the night. Then he lectured everyone for over an hour about his stupid rules. Then he forced us to stay in here even longer waiting for assignments. And now he wanted to reprimand me for playing tonsil hockey with Reed.

Well, two can play at the judgement game.

I put my hands on my hips and glared down at him. "You've just violated safe house rule number two."

"What?" He blinked as if in surprise.

"You grabbed me aggressively. I'd call that an act of violence."

He shook his head. "No, I only wanted to—"

"To threaten me? To intimidate me?"

"None of those things," he shouted, rocking back on his heels. He must have been too close to the edge of the step, because he fell backward and had to pinwheel his arms to find his balance again.

I bit the inside of my cheek to keep from laughing. Turning the tables on Sergeant Pain in the Ass was the most fun I'd had in days. Sniffing audibly, I added, "I don't enjoy being manhandled nor do I enjoy being lectured like a naughty child."

"You were dry humping in plain view of everyone." An edge crept back into his tone.

He had a point, but I sure as hell wouldn't give it to him.

"People can look away."

"They shouldn't have to." His nostrils flared. "You won't act like a two-dollar hooker in public again."

The authoritative tone in Dominic's voice hit a raw nerve. Anger and seduction were the only tools in my arsenal. Going with seduction, I fluttered my lashes at him. "What if I enjoy acting like a hooker?"

He sputtered clearly not knowing how to respond. I got the distinct impression, very few people ever challenged him.

"I've just added safe house rule twenty—no public

displays of affection," he announced with a smug lift of his chiseled chin.

I made a sound of exasperation. "Why do you have to have a rule for everything?"

Reed having finally realized I wasn't with the group, shouted, "Lee, come on!"

I cupped my mouth and called back, "Coming." I turned to glare at Dominic. "Are we done here?"

"No." Dominic folded his arms over his tactical vest. "You won't be excused until you understand that the rules maintain order and keep everyone safe." It might have been my imagination, but he sounded a tad defensive.

"And how is me kissing Reed unsafe?"

Dominic's expression tightened. "Because it might make some men want things they can't have." He probably intended his words to be a warning, but they sounded like a confession instead.

My stomach did a slow flip.

The air between us thickened with sexual tension.

"That's their problem," I said, licking my lips.

He tracked the motion of my tongue with an intensity that made it hard to breathe. "I don't think you understand how dangerous some of these men are."

Need and recklessness had me saying, "Maybe I like dangerous men watching me."

His breathing hitched, and he climbed a step. We were so close now, my next inhale was spiked with his cinnamon-scented breath.

We stared at each other without moving.

I had the feeling I'd taunted a predator to the point of attack. But instead of being afraid, I eagerly anticipated being feasted upon.

Dominic reached out and skimmed his fingers along my jaw.

A jolt of electricity crackled through both of us.

A groan escaped his lips. That strange connection between us grew stronger with every heartbeat.

I swayed forward, surrendering to the unseen force drawing us together.

His mouth was an inch from mine when an animalistic snarl had us both rearing back.

Over Dominic's shoulder, I saw Reed bounding up the bleacher steps.

Holy crap. I'd never seem him move so fast.

As if sensing a threat, Dominic spun around and held up his hand. "This doesn't concern you, Mr. Marshall—"

Reed smashed his fist into the sergeant's jaw.

I don't know who was in more shock, me or Dominic who stood there gaping at Reed.

"Reed!" I exclaimed in horror.

The sergeant caught Reed's next punch. "You've made a big mistake, Hippie." He squeezed Reed's fist so hard I heard popping joints.

"You're the one that made the mistake. Woof, mother-fucker," Reed growled.

Dominic's bronze face went pale. "What did you say?"

"You heard me, Dom." Reed reared back and smashed his forehead against Dominic's face.

Blood exploded from Dominic's nose, but the soldier continued to stand there as if struck dumb.

Reed tore his hand free and punched the sergeant again.

Dominic's head snapped back, his blood spraying my shirt.

"Stop it!" I tried to force my way between them.

"Stay back." Dominic put out his arm, keeping me from getting any closer.

Reed tossed his head, making his hood fall back. His long

sandy-blond hair flew around his face. "Don't worry, dirty dancer. A few punches won't hurt this Titan fucker."

The deep timber of Reed's voice and the darker hue of his eyes tipped me off to the fact that I was dealing with Reed's unstable alter ego.

"Not Reed," I said softly.

Reed flashed me a grin that was slightly feral.

Oh, no. My stomach dropped to my toes.

"Stand down," Dominic said under his breath. At first, I thought he was talking to me, but then I saw Darcy and Mike standing at the base of the bleachers. Both had their weapons drawn.

Crap. My heart pounded. *They're going to shoot Reed.* I had to stop this before things took a deadly turn.

Reed body-checked Dominic into the side of the aisle and reached for my hand. "Let's get out of here."

Dominic, moving faster than a striking cobra, intercepted the move. "Don't touch her."

Reed stepped right up into the massive soldier's face. "She's mine, Dom. My mate. And if you touch her again, I'll gut you where you stand."

Dominic returned his glare. "Return to your body, beast."

Beast?

Reed laughed. "Your orders don't work on me anymore. I'm free for the first time in my life. Free to fuck my mate." He winked at me over Dominic's shoulder. "Free to leave this place." He motioned around the room. "And free to avenge the deaths of my brothers."

Oh, God. He's totally insane.

"I won't allow it." Dominic grabbed him around the neck and squeezed.

Reed didn't help his cause by laughing. "My mate will never forgive you if you murder me."

"Stop!" I grabbed the back of Dominic's arm and tried to break his kung fu grip.

Reed made a choking sound, his face purpling.

He's going to strangle Reed. Panic had me grabbing my knife and pressing it against Dominic's throat. "Let Reed go."

Dominic swiveled his head to look at me. "You'd threaten my life over this beast?" The betrayal in his eyes shouldn't have stung, but it did.

"Let him go," I demanded, the knife trembling in my shaking hand. There was no way I'd actually slit his throat, and I sensed he knew that.

Dominic cursed and roughly tossed Reed down the steps.

Reed tumbled five rows and landed panting in the aisle.

I side-stepped Dominic and rushed down to him. "Are you okay?"

Nodding, Reed sat up. He tried to say something, but it came out a croak.

No wonder. The skin around his throat was swelling and bruising.

Dominic's boots thumped on the steps behind me.

We have to get out of here. "Can you walk?"

"Yeah," Reed answered hoarsely, pushing himself to his feet. He glared up at Dominic, but I was not about to let them fight again.

"Come on," I grabbed his hand and tugged him down the bleachers. As we descended, I noticed the gym was empty of everyone except the two soldiers who awaited us at the bottom. I tensed, waiting for Darcy and Mike to make a move, but they only watched us.

Their menacing glares put a chill down my spine. By attacking their sergeant, we'd crossed a dangerous line.

"You are nothing but a two-dollar hooker," Darcy sneered.

I blinked, realizing she'd overheard my conversation with Dominic. *How is that even possible?*

Reed didn't seem the slightest bit concerned about the soldiers. He shoved them out of the way and pulled me toward the back door.

"Wait..." If we went out that door, there'd be no coming back.

We'll be exiled.

A quick look back at Mike and Darcy's angry faces confirmed we already were.

My body went stiff with dread as I let Reed drag me through the door.

Where will we go? How will we possibly survive out there on our own?

We stepped out into icy rain that quickly soaked us to the bone.

As I shivered, Reed tilted his face up to the storm clouds and let out a dark laugh.

Only then did it really hit me. *Oh, God. I've traded my best chance of survival to be with a madman.*

❊ 7 ❊

HUNTER

I've always loved storms and this one was no exception. I relished the booming sound of thunder, the electric flash of lightning, and the musty scent of ozone and wet earth. Even the icy rain was a soothing balm to my cuts and bruises.

If I'd been in my old body, I could have shifted and healed those minor injuries in seconds. But I'd gladly endure the slow human healing process to escape Dom's control. That moment in the gym when Dom realized who he was dealing with was fucking priceless.

Laughing, I ripped off the sweatshirt I was wearing and tossed it into the mud. Then I did an all over body shake. The action wasn't as satisfying in this new body as it would have been in my old one, but that didn't bother me either.

Nothing could really bother me after having gotten the best of my former handler. It felt fucking amazing to see the horrified look on Dom's face when I made my big reveal.

Sure, it might have been smarter to keep Dom in the dark about my soul jumping abilities, but fuck that. I wanted him to know what I was capable of. I wanted to fuck with his head. Even more, I wanted him to fear me.

In all the years we'd been paired as beast and handler, I'd never seen him afraid. Not even during those FUBAR missions when death seemed inevitable.

I didn't think the merciless bastard was even capable of fear until a few minutes ago. The moment Lee pulled a knife on him up in the bleachers, I'd glimpsed it in his eyes.

He wasn't afraid of her actually using the weapon. A slit throat was nothing to a Titan like him. But he feared her turning against him.

And, as he'd taught me long ago, exploiting an enemy's fear was the surest path to defeating them.

Lee is the key to destroying Dom.

I gave my mate a savage grin.

Her forlorn expression cut me to the bone.

She's upset.

The same primitive instincts that drew me to claim her, demanded I ease her distress. *She's cold. I need to get her dry.*

"This way," I said, pulling her around the side of the school building. She seemed a bit dazed as I led her through the playground and into a cluster of long picnic tables protected by an overhanging roof. "Now we're out of the rain."

She gave me a jerky nod. Her eyes were too wide. Her skin too pale.

Maybe she's worried about the infected attacking us out here. I tried to put her mind at ease. "We're safe inside the school grounds." I motioned at the twelve-foot wrought-iron fence that ran the perimeter of the school.

"I know," she said, through chattering teeth. Her lips were taking on a bluish hue.

It's too cold for her out here. Cursing, I realized what a selfish bastard I'd been in bringing her outside. I'd only wanted to be alone with her for a few minutes without Dom or any of those irritating humans interrupting us. "Let's go back inside and get you warm." I headed toward the closest door that opened to the hallway near the kitchen.

It was locked. *Fuck.* Of course, it was locked. I yanked at the handle wishing I had a fraction of my beast strength in this body.

Lee touched my shoulder. "We can't go back inside."

"Not this way." I hid my annoyance with a shrug. "We'll have to walk back to the gymnasium door."

"We can't." She let out a deep breath. "Maybe we can find shelter in one of the surrounding buildings." She motioned around the front of the school.

"It wouldn't be wise to leave," I said slowly. *Doesn't she know hordes of infected are gathered around the front gates?*

"But we have no choice. We broke like ten of Dominic's stupid rules. He'll never let us back in now." She tried to laugh, but it sounded like a sob instead.

Is that the reason she's upset? "Of course, he will. In fact, he'll beg us to come back." Dom needed me, and as I'd just discovered, he needed her too.

She forced a smile. "He doesn't seem the begging type."

I snorted. "Definitely not. But he'll want us to stay. You'll have to trust me on this. He and I go back a long way." *Too long.*

She blinked. "What do you mean? How can you possibly know Dominic?"

I rubbed the knot blooming on the back of my head not knowing how to explain my fucked up relationship with Dom. "It's complicated."

Even though I'd only known my mate for a short while, I could tell my response irritated her. Her full lips thinned, and her brown eyes sparked with irritation. "Reed—"

"I'm not Reed," I growled, yanking her to my chest.

"I don't understand what's happening with you." She licked her lips nervously. "Do you have multiple personalities or something?"

"Or something." The sight of her pink tongue sent a shock of lust through my body. A sudden plan to warm her took shape.

"Let me teach you the difference between Reed and me." I bent my head and licked a drop of rain from the side of her neck.

She shivered, and I knew it wasn't from a chill.

"Would Reed kiss you like this?"

I claimed her mouth in a brutal kiss, loving the way her tongue danced with mine.

Within seconds we were both panting and moving restlessly against each other.

"Would he?" I growled against her lips.

"No," she moaned. Her eyes were dilated and unfocused.

Fuck. It'd been days since I'd been able to touch her. While Reed had been restrained in the nurse's office, I'd soul jumped into several other male bodies. However, each attempt to get Lee's attention had failed. It seemed she wasn't interested in any guy except for Reed. *And Dom.*

That thought filled me with jealous fury. *He'll never touch her. She's mine.*

Driven to stake my claim again, I scooped her up and unceremoniously dropped her on top of the closest picnic table. Then I tore off her shirt so fast the buttons zinged past my head and the plastic lighter in her shirt pocket flew out.

She wasn't wearing a bra. *Fuck.* I couldn't get her nipples in my mouth fast enough.

"We shouldn't," she moaned. "What if—"

I bit down hard enough to make her shudder.

"Oh, screw it." She fell back across the table. "We're probably going to die soon, anyway."

"Not going to happen." I'd go to the grave before allowing harm to come to her. I moved my attention to her other nipple.

She arched off the table as I licked and sucked. "Oh, God. That's good."

"I know what'd be even better." Needing to taste her, I kissed my way down her body. I took a moment to lave her belly button ring as that sexy piece of jewelry always cranked my lust into high gear. Then I licked down to the waistband of her jeans and tried to rip them off. The fucking things were plastered to her wet skin.

Laughing at my frustration, Lee kicked off her sneakers and shimmied out of her pants.

The moment she was bared to me, I dropped to my knees on the cold cement. "Would Reed make you come like this?" I buried my head between her legs and impaled her with my tongue. Her intoxicating honeyed taste was just as incredible as I remembered.

She shrieked, begging me for more.

I'll give her more. Gripping her ass in my hand, I licked my way up to her clit and suckled hard.

She came with a scream that was swallowed by the storm.

"Would he?" I demanded, sliding two fingers inside her.

"No," she cried. "Oh, God. Yes, right there."

I dragged her ass further down to the edge of the table and set to work using my mouth and fingers to bring her to orgasm after orgasm.

"Yes!" She rocked against my mouth. Her fingers dug into the back of my hair, pressing painfully against my most recent injury, but I could give a fuck. I'd burn alive on a pyre if it would bring her pleasure.

I bit down on her clit and she came again, her piercing screams followed by a rumble of thunder. Pushing myself to my feet, I yanked down the waistband of the sweatpants I was wearing and freed myself.

As I aligned our bodies, I felt a pang of regret that I could never mate her with my old body. My barbed cock would savage her.

But this... This human cock would bring her pleasure.

With a punch of my hips, I slammed home.

Incredible. My eyes rolled back as I seated deep inside her body. Her slick inner muscles clenched down on me so tightly, it took all my self-control not to explode inside her.

She hissed her approval and locked her legs around my waist. "Fuck me, Not Reed."

A jolt of masculine satisfaction pulsed through me. *She understands now.* Grinning, I thrust into her so hard and fast her large breasts slapped together.

"More!" Lee cried.

I drove into her over and over, fighting my body's burning demands. As lust cranked tighter and tighter inside me, I dropped my hand between us and worked her clit.

She went rigid.

Knowing she was close, I rubbed her harder and angled my hips so my cock reached that inner spot that drove her wild.

She let out a keening sound.

A bolt of lightning strobed the playground. A male watched us from the swings.

I didn't need to see his face to know it was Dom.

Let the bastard watch.

I pinched Lee's clit.

She exploded with a piercing shriek that might have temporarily cost me my hearing. So fucking worth it though.

I fell forward over her and after three frenzied thrusts I came so hard I might have blacked out.

It took her pressing against my chest for me to realize I

was crushing her. Mumbling an apology, I rocked back on my heels. My knees nearly gave out and I had to catch myself with the edge of the table.

"I think I like your multiple personalities," she said through panting breaths.

She looked so fucking beautiful with her damp hair tangled around her and her skin flushed from her orgasms. It also gave me a rush to see my cum smearing her trembling thighs.

"Christ, you didn't even wear a condom," Dom shouted, striding toward us. "You could have impregnated her."

Lee bolted upright. "What the actual fuck?"

Dom continued. "And you two just violated rule of survival number three, be aware of your surroundings at all times. What if I'd been a Biter?"

"Oh, God. You were watching us!" Lee exclaimed.

"I thought you liked dangerous men watching you," Dom quipped, stepping into view. Only someone who knew him as well as I did could tell the Titan was deeply affected by what he'd seen. Although he didn't outwardly show it, he was aroused as fuck.

To her credit, Lee didn't cringe away from his heated gaze. Instead, she pushed herself off the table and stared at him in challenge. "You're not one of them."

Dom's pained expression came and went so fast she probably didn't notice it, but I did. And I savored it.

Lee crossed her arms over her breasts. "And I can't get pregnant by the way."

Both Dom and I gawked at her in surprise.

She yanked my sweatpants over my cock and let the elastic snap me hard. "Don't pretend like you don't know that."

"Right," I said, with a nod. It was one of a million things I needed to learn about my mate.

Dom's eyes glazed over as he watched her bend down to grab her pants.

I stepped between them, trying to block his view. "What do you want?"

"To talk," he said, his gaze fixed on Lee.

Still naked, she dropped to her knees to fish the lighter out from under one of the picnic tables.

Dom swallowed hard.

I made a warning noise in my throat, trying to draw his focus to me.

He continued staring at her as she threw on her pants and knotted her shirt under her breasts.

Fuck. I'd have to find her something else to wear if I didn't want to fight off every male in the fucking school.

"Eyes on me," I growled to my former handler. It felt good to give him orders for once.

Seeming to wake from a trance, Dom blinked and cleared his throat. "Corporal Ross is waiting to give you your assignment, Ms. Walker."

Lee looked at him in disbelief. "You want us to stay?"

"For now..." He gave her a dark knowing look.

She went still. "You heard Reed and I talking all the way at the top of the bleachers?"

"I have excellent hearing," he replied.

"And your soldiers also overheard us talking at the top of the bleachers?"

Dom's top lip curled. "They have excellent hearing too."

I rolled my eyes. Titan soldiers had nearly as enhanced hearing as us shifters. No doubt he'd heard Lee's pleasured cries over the thunder and tracked us here.

"Go speak with Corporal Ross," Dom ordered.

Lee frowned, looking as if she would refuse.

"I'll be in shortly," I told her, dragging her in for one more kiss. I didn't release her until her lips were puffy and the vein in Dom's forehead throbbed.

Savoring his jealousy, I pinched her ass. "Go on, dirty dancer."

She gave me a look of mock outrage.

"Or I can throw you back down on here for round two." I patted the top of the table.

She flipped me off and turned to walk away. She didn't get more than a few feet before spinning around. "Do you promise not to hurt him?"

I wasn't sure if her question was directed at Dom or me, but we both answered, "Yes."

Seeming satisfied, she rounded the side of the building and disappeared from sight.

That left me alone with the male I'd wanted to kill for the last three years.

"So," I said, glaring at him. "What the fuck do you want to talk about?"

He returned my scowl. "Let's start with you explaining how you got inside that hippie's body."

❧ 8 ❧

LEE

Not trusting Reed and Dominic to keep their promise, I flattened my back against the wall on the other side of them.

The roof protected me from the rain, but without Reed and my hormones keeping me warm, my internal temperature seemed to drop fast. It certainly didn't help that the brick wall was freezing, and I'd had to tie up my shirt since Reed had torn off most of the buttons.

What were we thinking having sex out here?

As much as I hated to admit it, Dominic was right to chew our asses out.

What if a zombie had stumbled on us while we'd been out of our minds with lust? We couldn't let our guard down and ignore our surroundings like that.

Well, I hadn't totally been ignoring my surroundings. Somehow, I'd known Dominic was watching us. And I'd continued having sex with Reed anyway.

In fact, I'd enjoyed knowing Dominic was watching. *God.* That sounded so messed up. But some part of me really got off on having the sergeant there. Just imagining him joining in had made me orgasm harder than ever.

What's happening to me? Just three days ago, I'd been a virgin and now I craved multiple lovers.

Maybe I was going crazy like Reed. Instead of hearing voices, I'd turned into a sexual deviant.

Rubbing my arms, I strained to hear the guys' conversation over the drumming rain.

Reed's laugh was deeper and colder than normal. "It seems my twin brother isn't the only one with special abilities."

Twin brother? Reed didn't have any siblings. All he had was his mom and after she'd died in the car accident, there had been no other family to take him in. That's why Gran had opened our home to him.

Dominic made a frustrated sound. "Your unconscious body has been lying on the office floor for days."

His body?

Reed scoffed. "You can dispose of it."

"You will return to it," Dominic's order was laced in steel.

"No."

"You are my beast."

Beast?

Reed's voice dropped lower. "I'm going to kill you."

It was Dominic's turn to laugh. "If you were going to, you would have already."

What? I was so damn confused.

Reed sounded defensive. "I'm not giving you a quick death. I want you to suffer the way I've suffered."

Dominic let out a heavy sigh. "This is about Afghanistan."

"Yes, it's about fucking Afghanistan. You killed my brothers," Reed shouted.

Afghanistan? Reed, like me, had never left Arizona, and he certainly didn't have a bunch of brothers that Dominic could have killed.

Reed took a shuddering breath as if to compose himself. "But my revenge will have to wait. Right now I need your help keeping my mate alive. The city is FUBAR. I've gone over every mile looking for a safer place to take her and found nothing."

"Wh-what?" Dominic sputtered. "How did you see anything? You've been lying on the floor—"

Reed interrupted. "I told you. I'm not bound to that body anymore."

"You'll return to it or—"

"Or what, Dom? You'll kill this body?" Reed chuckled. "If I don't die immediately, then I'll jump into another. Maybe one of your Titan soldiers. Would you like to die by their hand? It's more than you deserve."

Are they both insane? It sounded as if Dom had drunk some of Reed's crazy Kool-Aid.

A chill wracked me, and I had to fight to keep my teeth from chattering.

"Just tell me what's going on out there, Hunter."

Hunter? That was what Reed had called the voice in his head. The hair on the back of my neck stood on end.

Reed let out a sigh, "There are a few pockets of survivors, most of them holed up in buildings scattered around town. Hordes of infected roam the streets. Some hordes range in the hundreds. Others in the thousands."

Dominic cursed.

"Alpha Diaz has been sending his enforcers to pick up survivors in the south."

I inhaled sharply. *Is Reed talking about Javier Diaz?*

"That's the bastard who killed Jen?"

Who's Jen?

"Yes," Reed confirmed. "He has a heavily fortified compound in the south valley and enough weapons and enforcers to take out the army base, not that he has to at this point."

Dominic's voice went low. "Why? What happened on base?"

"I have no fucking idea. But it was a bloodbath. All that's left are infected, and..."

"And?" Dominic repeated.

"These other creatures. I don't know what the fuck they are. They looked like zombies, but they're fast and loud. Base was covered with them."

"Those must be the Howlers," Dominic said slowly. "The colonel warned me about them during my briefing."

"Well, the asshole should have taken his own advice—"

Dominic interrupted. "If they were overrun, the colonel would have gone underground. The bunker is designed to sustain an entire brigade for years. They'll regroup with the rest of AMBER and take out the infected."

"I wouldn't be so sure. There were Titans among the dead."

What are titans? The guys kept using that term.

"No," Dominic said emphatically. "You must have been mistaken."

"There's no mistake. I saw the remains of Henris and Owsinski. Those things... those Howlers turned them into Sloppy Joes."

Dominic cursed again. "I need you to go to the bunker."

"I can't."

"That's not a request, beast. It's an order. Go back to your old body, shift, and find the colonel."

As Dominic's shout rang in my ears, I surrendered to the impossible truth. Reed was possessed by someone else... this

Hunter. And he and Dominic knew each other. My hands shook as I tried to process what that meant.

"Fuck you, Dom," Hunter-possessed-Reed shouted. "I really fucking can't. I'm... stuck in here."

Dominic asked the same question on my mind, "What the hell does that mean?"

"It means I'm trapped. Initially, I could jump in and out of Reed. But after my last soul jump, I got locked in here." His voice climbed a few octaves. "Ah... shut up, cocksucker. I'm sick of being in your body, too."

"Are you talking to the hippie?" Dominic asked.

"Yeah. We're taking turns being in control, but if he doesn't shut the fuck up right now, I won't give him his turn." It sounded as if Hunter-possessed-Reed smacked himself in the head.

"So, you can't jump into your old body," Dominic mused.

Hunter-possessed-Reed made a noise of agreement.

"But earlier you said if I killed you, you could jump into a new body," Dominic said slowly.

"It might free me, or I might die too," Hunter-possessed-Reed said, before shouting, "I didn't say we were going to kill you, cocksucker. Just be quiet and let the adults talk."

"We have to risk it," Dominic announced. The sound of one of his knives being unsheathed chilled my blood.

"No, Dom. Losing Reed would devastate my mate. I will not cause her pain."

"But you'll wear her lover's body like a damn suit?"

Hunter-Possessed-Reed sniffed. "That's different. And they aren't lovers. I'm the one mating her, not him." He cursed loudly. "Shut the fuck up, cocksucker. She belongs to me. It doesn't matter how long you've known each other."

"It sounds as if the hippie disagrees with you," Dominic said dryly.

"Whatever. We're working our shit out. The take home

here is that Reed lives, Lee is mine, and you're going to help keep us all alive."

"No," Dominic said in a clipped voice.

"Motherfucker, you owe me—" The sound of a man shouting in the distance interrupted him.

Dominic cursed. "Corporal Shaw needs assistance reinforcing the gate."

"I can help."

I missed whatever else was said because the men's voices faded out of earshot.

Shaken to my very soul, I made my way around the back of the school. My sneakers squelched in the mud and rain poured down my face, but I didn't even notice.

My brain felt as if it was going to explode as I tried to make sense of what I'd heard. A lot of it was too confusing to understand, but what I got was that Reed wasn't crazy. He was possessed by Hunter, who was Dominic's beast. Whatever the hell that meant. And Dominic wanted to free Hunter by killing Reed. And that was something I couldn't allow to happen.

But how can I stop him? And how can I stop Hunter from possessing Reed?

I didn't even know what I was dealing with. *Is Hunter a demon? Do I need a priest to do an exorcism or something?*

As I stumbled through the rain, my heart ached for Reed. I felt terrible that I'd assumed he'd lost his mind when in actuality he'd been battling a demon.

A demon I'd had sex with.

A sick feeling washed over me as my mind played back every intimate moment we'd shared in nauseating high definition. It'd been the demon who'd kissed me, gone down on me, and screwed me like a wild man. Not Reed.

Bile rose in my throat as I realized it'd also been the

demon who I'd fucked in the locker room and the demon who'd taken my virginity three nights ago.

Oh, God.

I should have known. The way Reed talked and acted was so out of character. And even his eyes had looked different.

I stopped outside the door to the gym. Someone had closed it. Probably Dominic who'd likely enjoyed watching me being railed by his beast.

My breath came faster as revulsion and shame turned my stomach. Tears welled in my eyes, but I blinked them away along with the disgust and self-recrimination. Instead, I focused on the raw burning emotion radiating from below my rib cage up to the center of my chest.

Rage I could handle. Rage I knew well.

Reed and I had been violated. The demon had taken something from us we could never get back. And I didn't know how, but I was going to make it pay for that. Dominic was a co-conspirator as far as I was concerned, and he was going to pay too. Just as soon as I figured out what we were dealing with.

I clenched my hands into fists and pounded on the door.

It flew open, nearly smacking me in the face.

"Finally. I've been waiting for you, hooker," Darcy said with her signature sneer.

"And you can wait a little longer, bitch." My anger gave me the strength to shove past the taller, far more muscular woman.

Darcy's expression turned deadly. "What did you just call me?"

"I'm pretty sure you heard me the first goddamn time since you have excellent hearing."

Her fingers tightened reflexively along the sniper rifle she carried. "Dominic and I should have left you to die."

"Maybe you should have," I muttered, stalking by her. I

didn't have the emotional bandwidth to fight with her. Besides, there was something I needed to see. Leaving a puddle of water in my wake, I marched across the basketball court, yanked open one of the double doors, and stalked down the hallway in search of the demon's body.

❧ 9 ❧

LEE

The school was as quiet as a graveyard. As I moved through the empty hallway, I caught glimpses of people sleeping in the classrooms. Under Dominic's rules, all civilians not on patrol had to be in their assigned classrooms until dawn.

Screw Dominic and his rules.

He wanted to kill Reed to free his beast and I would not let that happen.

My wet sneakers squeaked on the speckled linoleum floor as I picked up the pace. Dominic had mentioned that Hunter's body was on an office floor. He had to be talking about the principal's office. Dominic had taken up residence there, while his soldiers turned the nearby teachers' lounge into their sleeping quarters, not that any of them seemed to sleep.

I tensed knowing that any minute one of the soldiers could come through the hallway and try to force me back into a classroom.

The lanterns on the floor flickered as if in warning. Despite knowing better, I glanced at the tree mural on the wall. If anything, it looked even creepier than before. Until now, I hadn't noticed that each red leaf handprint bore the name of a child.

Are any of those children still alive?

Trying not to shudder, I rushed past the lockers and came to another set of double doors. I cautiously pushed one of the blue doors open not knowing whether I'd find a soldier patrolling the other side.

Thankfully, the hallway was clear. Feeling as if I'd lucked out, I stepped through the doorway and caught sight of my reflection in the glass of a large trophy case.

My God. I look like hell. My long hair hung in a limp, wet, tangle around my pale, makeup-free face. It really brought out the dark shadows bruising the underside of my bloodshot eyes. I looked like a dumpster diving hobo. Scratch that. I looked like something a dumpster diving hobo would find on the bottom of their shoe.

I started to pinch color in my cheeks, before shaking off the rush of vanity. *Screw my appearance.* For the first time in years, the survival of my family wasn't tied to my sex appeal. Instead, Reed's survival depended on how quickly I could come up with a plan to save him. Too bad I hadn't been the brainy one in the family. Eden had that honor, not that she'd actually used her intelligence for anything other than getting into trouble.

As if my thoughts had conjured her up, my sister stepped out of the library down the hall. She seemed completely unaware of me as she balanced a clear plastic baggie filled with syringes and glass vials on top of a stack of bloody towels.

"Hey, Edie."

She spun around so quickly the baggie nearly slipped off the towels. Securing it with one hand, she gave me a surprised look. "Lee, what are you doing here?"

"I'd ask you the same question." As I moved closer to the library door, the acrid smell of cat urine made my eyes water. "Another cat fight?" It seemed Eden was constantly trying to keep the felines and other animals from killing each other.

"Kind of." She quickly closed the door and flattened her back against it. "I'm headed to the nurse's office to return the pain meds and get more bandages for... Clyde."

"Which one is he?" My sister had given me a rundown of all the animals in the library, but I hadn't paid much attention. I really didn't give half a shit now, but there was something about Eden's behavior that triggered my alarm bells.

What's she up to?

"He's the ferret," she said, not budging from her position in front of the door. "He got into it with Summer. She's the calico that Rosie likes so much."

Forgetting about Reed for a moment, I moved closer to the door. "I'd like to see him."

She surprised me by stepping aside. "Fine. Although I don't know why you'd want to. It's not as if you've ever cared about the animals before."

Ignoring the scorn in her voice, I tried to turn the door handle. It wouldn't move. "It's locked."

"Really?" Eden wore a look of feigned surprise. "And I don't have the key with me either. Dang. Looks as if I'm going to have to have a soldier open it for me again."

I knew my sister too damn well to fall for her act. "Edie." I gave her the big sister glare. "What's really going on?"

She gave me a wide-eyed look of innocence. "Nothing, sissy." When I continued glaring, her gaze narrowed. "You'll just have to trust me."

I exhaled heavily, feeling frustration welling up inside me. I should have been able to trust her. I should have been able to confide in her all the crazy shit that was going on with Reed and Dominic and the demon. But we'd always had an adversarial relationship. Maybe we would have been closer if our entire family hadn't been wiped out in a single horrible night so many years ago and I hadn't been tasked with looking after her. But I'd taken that responsibility seriously. Maybe too seriously.

As I studied the annoyed expression on her face, I realized I was the Avi to her Zara. And much like Zara couldn't stand to be around her eldest brother, Eden couldn't stand to be around me. The knowledge shouldn't have stung as much as it did, but my emotions were raw and I was exhausted. "You know I'm only on your ass all the time because I love you."

"Maybe you could love me a little less," she groused. "I'm an adult, capable of making decisions for myself."

"Are you?" If only I could trust in her decisions. But time and time again, I was left cleaning up her messes and bailing her ass out of jail. And yet, if I didn't ease up on her, I knew intuitively she'd keep pulling away.

Eden rolled her eyes. "Whatever. Anyway, I have to return these meds. Sharon wants all the narcotics tightly controlled." She patted the plastic baggie.

As I stared at the medicine bottles inside, I remembered Reed saying the meds Sharon gave him stopped him from hearing Hunter. An idea flashed in my mind. I reached out and snatched the baggie from her.

Eden tried to grab it back and dropped her stack of towels. "What the hell?"

"I need more pain meds for Reed." I peered at the syringes and bottles inside the baggie.

Shaking her head, she picked up her towels. "Those are hard core, Lee. You can't give him any of those narcotics. Besides Sharon will have my ass if I don't return them. Those are Bernard's meds and I wasn't exactly supposed to take them in the first place."

I faked a gasp. "Do you mean you stole them from her? And here I thought you were so trustworthy."

She grimaced. "Just give me the bag back, Lee."

"No." With these, Reed could suppress the demon, maybe indefinitely.

Eden didn't look happy. "That's really addictive stuff. It's not something to mess around with."

"You'll just have to trust me," I said, throwing her words back at her.

The brat gave me a dirty look. "I'm going to tell Sharon you have her meds. She'll come after you."

"She can get in line." I wasn't scared of the nurse, or Darcy, or Dominic, or Hunter. Especially not with this. I clutched the baggie to my chest.

Eden huffed and stalked off.

Feeling relieved that I had at least some kind of plan, I followed her toward the eastern wing of the school until the hallway branched. As she continued toward the nurse's office, I took a right and headed toward the front entrance of the school.

The glass doors were closed, but I could see multiple flashlights bobbing around in the darkness outside. If my luck held, all the soldiers would be outside reinforcing the gate or whatever the hell Dominic said they were doing.

I'd just relaxed when Mike stepped out of the teachers' lounge and into my path.

The blond soldier looked almost as intimidating as Dominic as he loomed over me in his army uniform. "Ms. Walker, you need to be in your assigned classroom."

Thinking fast, I said, "Oh, well I was helping Eden look for you."

His suspicious expression morphed into one of surprise. "She's looking for me?"

"Yes, she needed your help with something." And I wasn't

totally lying. Eden told me she needed a soldier to let her into the library, even though I'd bet my only pair of jeans she'd had the key on her. "She's headed to the nurse's office."

"Oh," he glanced over my shoulder. The eagerness in his blue eyes made me blurt out, "Is there a rule that soldiers and civilians can't be together?"

His expression fell. "Yes."

"Oh, that's too bad because my sister is totally into you." I winked. *Take that you lying brat*. "I'll head back to my classroom."

"You do that," Mike said in a choked voice. Then the man practically zoomed around me in his haste to hunt down my sister.

Chuckling, I stepped behind the empty reception desk and approached the principal's office. The mini blinds covering the windowpane in the door were closed and the room was dark. Still, I turned the handle slowly.

I half expected the door to be locked, but it wasn't. I quickly yanked it open, stepped inside, and closed the door behind me. The office was pitch black and of course I didn't have a flashlight.

Crap.

But I had one of Reed's small plastic lighters. Shoving the baggie under my arm, I fumbled around in my pockets until I found it. Congratulating myself on having picked it up after it'd fallen out of my shirt outside, I tried to ignite a spark.

Click. Click. Click. Oh, come on!

The fourth time was the charm. Holding the small flame out in front of me, I swung it around the room. *What a letdown*. There wasn't much of anything in here. Just an L-shaped desk cluttered with stacks of papers, a wall of metal filing cabinets, and two chairs parked near a door that read 'Principal.'

Getting warmer, I told myself. As I crossed the small space, I caught a whiff of vanilla from an unlit candle sitting on the desk. The scent, one of my favorites, made me homesick. Wondering if I'd ever be able to return to my old life, I grabbed the candle and lit it. The much bigger flame brightened my mood and the room.

Pocketing the lighter, I re-secured the baggie under my arm and carried the candle over to the real principal's office. Holding my breath, I opened it.

Inside was a massive office, roughly half the size of the classroom I'd been sleeping in. Other than the shiny framed diplomas mounted on the wall, it looked nothing like any principal's office I'd ever been in. I whistled under my breath at the expensive-looking ebony desk with matching floor to ceiling bookcases. There was even a stained-glass Tiffany lamp sitting on a side table by a long black leather couch.

What would a principal even do with a couch that size? Sleep on it? Maybe there was a mini bar under the desk too.

Scoffing under my breath, I scanned the rest of the space. *Dominic said Hunter's body lay on the office floor, right?*

My stomach sank as I realized Dominic could have been referring to another location. *Dammit. Maybe he meant one of the office buildings down the street.* Feeling more and more let down, I carried my candle closer to the desk. Dozens of knives were lined up over the top of the black wood. The wickedly sharp blades gleamed in the candlelight.

The weapons, along with the open bag of cinnamon hard candy sitting on the desk, were a jolting reminder I was invading the private space of a dangerous man.

Time to go.

I'd just backed away, when I spied something large crammed behind the leather executive chair.

What's that?

As I stepped around the desk, I realized there was a green blanket draped over something that looked to be a body.

I gasped when I spotted a giant foot, larger than a car tire, peeking out from underneath the blanket.

Oh, God. Is this Hunter?

Holding my breath, I set the candle and baggie down on the desk. Then I knelt down and lifted the blanket. I don't know what I expected to find under there. Maybe a horned, red-skinned demon or a bestial-looking monster. Instead, I came face-to-face with an attractive man whose unique features were strangely familiar.

It was crazy because there was no way I'd ever seen him before. It's not like I could have ever forgotten seeing someone with ombre shoulder-length hair that went from strawberry-blond, to burgundy, to dark black. And I couldn't have forgotten that heavy dark brow, prominent cheekbones, and rugged chin. The guy oozed so much testosterone it surprised me that his enormous body was hairless. Even more surprising was the fact that his broad chest rose and fell evenly.

Given the way Dominic had been discussing him, I'd assumed Hunter was dead. But he was very much alive, and he had to be over ten-feet-tall.

What the hell is he?

The blanket slipped out of my trembling hands and fell onto his face.

I tensed waiting for him to open his eyes.

When he didn't, I leaned over and whispered, "Hello," like an idiot.

He didn't respond.

I pushed the blanket aside and patted his smooth face trying to wake him. When that didn't work, I peeled one of his eyelids open.

A metallic gold iris stared sightlessly back at me.

Wow. He definitely wasn't human. I should have been

terrified, but once again I was struck by a strong sense of familiarity.

I know him.

Driven by a strange urge, I pushed up his top lip revealing a mouthful of long, wickedly, sharp teeth. His elongated canines would make any vampire-wannabe pant in desire.

Is he a demon-vampire?

Unable to shake the strange compulsion to touch him. I shoved the blanket down and traced my hands down the smooth, golden skin of his chest. I'd never seen a guy as ripped as him. I swear his muscles had muscles. Not even Dominic or any body builder I'd ever seen could hold a candle to his physique. He even had a twelve-pack. I counted his abs a second time just to confirm it.

The blanket, pooled at his waist and stopped my exploration. I chewed my bottom lip with indecision. Touching someone without their permission was wrong. But then again, Hunter possessed Reed to have sex with me, so... I lifted the blanket and did a double take.

What the hell is that?

The huge appendage laying between the demon's muscular thighs was well over a foot long, as thick as my calf, and studded from base to tip with strange bumps. Fascinated, I ran my hand over them. The bumps felt like smooth, fleshy protrusions if I stroked downward, but if I slid my hand upward, they became spikes that dug painfully into my skin.

Holy crap. No way was that thing ever getting inside me.

"That's one way to rouse a male from a coma, Ms. Walker."

Shit. I twisted around so fast I nearly fell over Hunter's body.

Dominic stood directly behind me, close enough to slit my throat.

10

LEE

On an embarrassment scale from one to ten, having Dominic find me stroking the cock of the comatose demon in his office was an eleven. My face flamed, and I jerked my hand back to my side. "I-I didn't see you there."

How can a man his size move so quietly?

"Clearly," Dominic said in a dry voice. "This space is off limits to civilians. What are you doing here?"

"I..." I struggled to come up with a plausible story. "... I was looking for you and I stumbled across this... guy."

"And you stopped to fondle his genitals?"

Oh, God. My face felt as if it might actually catch fire. "N-no. Um. I don't think he's human."

"Very astute, Ms. Walker. However, that doesn't explain why you were assaulting him."

"I beg your pardon."

He arched a dark brow. "Did he give you permission to touch his penis?"

I rolled my eyes. "I'm pretty sure the demon won't mind."

Dominic's top lip curled slightly, and I had the distinct impression he was toying with me. "He's not a demon."

"Then what is he?"

"A biologically enhanced soldier," he said matter-of-factly, as if finding a ten-foot-tall, muscle-packed guy with metallic eyes, fangs, and a mace for a cock was no big deal.

"Enhanced to do what? Destroy vaginas?" I waved down at Hunter's crotch.

Dominic's cough sounded suspiciously like a muffled laugh. "No. He was engineered by army scientists for speed, strength, stealth, and regenerative capabilities."

As his words sunk in, I realized Cami had been right with her conspiracy theories all along. *The military is doing crazy genetic experiments.* Too bad she wasn't alive to gloat about it. "Are there more soldiers like him?"

Dominic's jaw locked and some emotion I couldn't place swept across his face. "No. Not like him."

Thank God for small favors, as Gran used to say. I released the breath I was holding. A million questions bubbled into my mind, but before I could ask one, Dominic took a step closer.

"Why did you want to see me?"

"Um." *Dammit.* I had to think of something. Flustered, I rubbed my clammy hands on my jeans. *What plausible reason can I give?* "I-I... um... just wanted to apologize for what you saw outside." It sounded lame to my own ears, but it was the best I could come up with.

"Why?"

Yeah, why would I apologize? Feeling a rush of indignation, I jerked my chin up. "You're right. You should apologize for watching us."

He cocked his head to the side. "You invited me to watch you."

"I-I did not," I sputtered.

His eyes glinted with dark fire. "Didn't you?"

At once, I became all too aware that I was kneeling on the floor at his feet. It made me feel vulnerable and subservient, something I never wanted to feel with any man. *Especially this man.* I stood, anticipating that Dominic would move back.

He didn't.

We were six inches from each other, and I had to crane my neck back to glare at him. "Can you give me some space?"

"Why? You thought nothing of invading my space," he motioned around the room.

He has a point. I took a deep breath and mainlined his spicy-sweet cinnamon breath. His close proximity fogged my brain and a crazy amount of sexual tension charged the air between us.

As he stood there staring at me, an unwelcome wave of desire pulsed through my body, making my nipples pucker against the fabric of my tied shirt.

To his credit, Dominic's gaze never dipped from my face. "I know you overheard my conversation with Hunter. Is that why you came here?"

Crap. I could have played dumb, but I had a feeling Dominic could see right through my bullshit. Deciding the truth was my only option, I said, "I needed to see him."

"And touch him?" Dominic's mocking tone grated my nerves.

I lifted my chin. "Are you jealous?" As soon as the words left my mouth, I wanted to cram them back in.

"Do you want me to be?"

I shuddered, feeling suddenly breathless and achy between my legs. "Maybe," I confessed. *My God.* This man jumbled up my head and emotions so fast I had trouble concentrating on anything other than his spicy-sweet breath and the proximity of his huge muscular body.

He shifted closer and one of the daggers strapped to his

vest brushed against me. "Soldiers don't fraternize with civilians." It sounded as if he was reminding himself of that.

"Is that an army rule or one of your safe house rules?" I asked too breathlessly.

"Yes," he answered in that infuriating way of his.

"Well, you should tell that to the demon possessing my..." The word boyfriend got stuck in my throat. "...friend."

Dominic moved away faster than I could blink. One moment he was in my face, the next he was across the room grabbing a bottle of water from the side table.

What the hell? Maybe Hunter wasn't the only enhanced soldier. Although Dominic wasn't as large as the demon, he was plenty big at six-and-a-half feet. Dominic was also strong enough to stab through Dr. Bloom's skull as if it were made of Styrofoam and he moved faster than my eyes could track.

Does he have a monster cock too? My gaze dropped to the fly of his army fatigues not that I could see what was going on down there through the fabric. Visions of him sporting a spiked appendage similar to Hunter's made me clamp my thighs together.

Dominic rubbed the underside of his clean-shaven chin. "Hunter never demonstrated this ability before." I didn't like the hint of awe in his voice. Demon possession wasn't something to be excited about.

"We need to get Hunter out of Reed," I said, stating the obvious.

"Agreed."

"Without killing Reed," I added quickly.

Dominic frowned. "I don't know if there's another way."

"What do you mean?" I exploded. "You find another way. You're not killing my... you're not killing Reed."

Dominic shook his head. "You don't understand. Hunter is incredibly dangerous. In his natural form, I am his handler and he is completely under my control. But free of our bond he is a threat to every soldier and civilian in the school. I must return him to his body." I could tell by the clenching of his jaw he'd already decided.

I refused to accept it. "No. I won't allow you to hurt Reed."

The cold smirk on Dominic's face pissed me off.

Clearly, he didn't consider me a threat. I got it. Most guys discounted women, especially women that looked like me. Their mistake. I possessed skills that could bring the cockiest asshole to his knees. Tossing back my almost dry hair, I tried a different tool in my arsenal. "You heard what Hunter said. He won't return to his body. If you kill Reed, Hunter will only hijack a...." *What's that word he used? Oh, yeah.* "...a titan."

Dominic flinched. "He'll return to his body." He didn't sound convinced.

"Are you certain about that?" I snagged the baggie of medicine from the desk, walked over to Dominic, and snatched the bottle of water from his hand. Taking a swig, I lounged back on the sofa.

"That was mine," he said, his expression somewhere between indignant and amused.

"And now it's mine," I said, licking around the rim of the bottle.

His shell-shocked look delighted me.

Everyone, including me if I was being honest, was scared as hell of this guy. Throwing him off his game was all part of my strategy. I patted the baggie in my lap. "I have another idea."

Dominic glanced at the baggie and frowned. "I didn't peg you for a drug addict."

The scorn in his voice raised my hackles. "I'm not. Just listen, Sergeant Pain in the Ass."

His eyes narrowed. "Call me sir."

"Fine, Sir Pain in the Ass."

He gritted his teeth. "Ms. Walker, you will address me with respect."

Oh, looky. He had a big throbbing vein in his forehead now. It made me wonder about his package again. "Do you have a monster cock?"

He let out a rush of breath. "What?"

Crap. Did I actually say that out loud? Ugh. "Never mind. My plan is to dope Reed up on painkillers until we can figure out how to exorcize the demo—Hunter." I shook the baggie. "Reed said he can't hear Hunter's voice when he's on the drugs, so we'll keep him high."

Dominic pursed his lips as if considering the idea. "And what if we can't force Hunter out?"

"We'll get him out." Failure wasn't an option.

Dominic shook his head. "Such confidence in things you know nothing about."

"I'm a glass-half-full kind of gal," I said, lying through my teeth. I was a natural born pessimist.

"And Hippie is okay with your plan?"

"He will be," I replied. "And stop calling him that. He's not some long-haired, peace-loving druggie. Reed can man-up when he needs to."

"That was clear outside." An edge crept back into Dominic's tone.

Clearly, reminding him of Hunter-possessed-Reed and I boning wasn't making him happy. "Look, it was your demon who coerced me into sex." Not exactly true, but whatever. "Reed and I were virgins before Hunter took over his body."

Dominic smirked. "I have a hard time believing that."

That pissed me off. "Believe whatever you want." I stood up suddenly, sending the water bottle rolling onto the carpet. "You won't hurt Reed." I grabbed the bag of medicine and headed for the door. *Time for plan B*. Find Reed, inject him with the narcotics, and get the hell out of dodge. If the Blooms could break out and live long enough to get to their house and find their damn dog, then Reed and I could get out too. We just needed to find a safe place to hole up. Maybe we could even track down Danika —if she was still alive—and start a survival group of our own.

"Sit down, Ms. Walker."

I grabbed the door handle. "Goodbye, Sergeant Pain in the Ass."

"Sit down," Dominic shouted so loudly the diplomas on the wall shook.

Realizing that I may have pushed the sergeant too far, I spun around. The vein in his temple was doing the throbbing again and the tic in his jaw was working overtime. I sighed. Me fighting with Dominic wouldn't help Reed. I might as well try a friendly approach.

"Fine," I said stiffly. I walked back to the couch and sat.

The brackets of tension around Dominic's mouth eased. "From now on, you will refer to me as sir."

I rolled my eyes.

"As part of our bargain, you will park the attitude Ms. Walker."

"Our bargain?" I wasn't aware we were negotiating.

"I will not harm Reed, as long as Hunter is suppressed."

I let out a relieved breath. "Thank you."

"In return, you will follow my rules and every single one of my orders."

Every single order? I wet my lips. "Am I agreeing to be your sex slave?"

He inhaled sharply. "I told you. Soldiers don't fraternize with civilians."

I noticed he didn't completely answer the question, but I let it go. "Okay. I agree. And in return for me following your rules and orders, Reed stays alive, you'll let him stay in a room by himself, and you'll figure out a way to exorcize the demon."

His eyes narrowed. "He gets his own room?"

I shrugged. "It seems the least you can do as it was your demon... excuse me, enhanced soldier who possessed my lover."

Dominic's brow furrowed. "You said Reed wasn't your lover."

"Well, he wasn't, but now that we've crossed the line, there's no backing that truck up." Once I said the words, the truth of them hit me. I didn't want to go back to the platonic relationship Reed and I had before.

The knowledge shook me. Despite trying to avoid romantic entanglements all my life, I'd somehow ended up falling for my best guy friend. I adored Reed's selflessness, his quirky sense of humor, and the way he looked at me as if I could solve all the world's problems. Of course, I also loved his tight ass and the way he licked my—

"You'll end things with Hippie."

Dominic's declaration had me jumping to my feet. "What? No way."

"Did you or did you not agree to follow my orders?"

"The reasonable orders," I clarified.

"All. My. Orders." Dominic was suddenly in front of me.

I fell back into the sofa cushions, an undignified squeak escaping my lips. "How the hell do you move that fast?"

Ignoring my question, Dominic leaned down, so we were nose-to-nose. "If I tell you to jump, you jump. If I tell you to break up with your boyfriend, you break up with your boyfriend."

I returned his glare. "And if you tell me to get on my knees and suck your monster cock, am I supposed to do that too?"

His cinnamon-scented breath went choppy and the pupils

of his black as sin eyes exploded. "One day I'm going to punish you for your impertinence."

"I might like a good spanking," I murmured, my eyes dropping to his lips. He had gorgeous lips. The top one was bow-shaped and the bottom one was perfect nibbling size.

He cursed and flashed to the door. "It's time for you to go, Ms. Walker. I'm handling Reed and Hunter."

Not liking the sound of that, I pushed myself up, careful not to damage the baggie still clasped in my hand. "No. I'm going to talk to Reed and—"

Dominic reached over and snatched the baggie from me.

"Give that back."

Ignoring my outrage, he opened the door and waved me out. "Goodbye, Ms. Walker."

My anger vanished the moment I caught sight of the small admin office outside the door. "Oh my God!"

Reed lay on the floor next to the file cabinets. He was gagged, zipped tied, and appeared unconscious.

I gave Dominic a sharp look.

He shrugged. "I told you. I'm handling it."

11

REED

FML. Once again, I was trapped inside the darkness of my mind with the biggest alpha asshole in the universe.

It was as if I were starring in one of those B-horror movies I used to marathon watch on the weekends. But instead of devouring my soul like he was supposed to, the body snatcher had moved in, and wanted to become best buds.

Maybe I should have told him I'd beaten in the skull of my last best friend. But then again, Hunter was a pretty messed up dude and he'd probably like that.

I wanted to scream out all my rage and frustration at this fucked up situation, but it was pointless. Over the past three days, I'd learned that no amount of self-harm, screaming, threatening, bargaining, or begging would make Hunter go away. Sharon's pills were the only thing that did. But the effect was temporary and as soon as the meds were out of my system, Hunter was back in full force, doing what he loved to do best—complain about Dominic.

"Give it a rest, man," I pleaded.

Hunter ignored me, as usual. *"I can't believe that sneaky motherfucker got the drop on us like that."* As he shouted, the surrounding darkness slowly morphed into the inside of a large canvas tent.

Hunter often brought us to this dreamscape although I wasn't sure he did it intentionally. There wasn't much inside the army tent other than a ruggedized laptop set up on a card table, a folding chair, and two very uncomfortable looking sleeping cots.

The occasional boom of mortars detonating somewhere in the distance shook the olive-green tent every so often. The sound freaked me the hell out but seemed to comfort Hunter.

Expecting another bitchfest, I sprawled out on one of the cots.

Hunter paced around the table. *"How many times is Dom going to betray me?"*

There was no point in answering. Anything I said would only crank Hunter up even more. To say his feelings about Dominic were complex was an understatement. Over the last three days, he'd gone from boasting of Dominic's heroics during their special ops missions to outlining all the ways he planned to kill the sergeant. I didn't know if Hunter was aware of the love-hate bromance he had going on with Dominic, but I certainly wouldn't be the one to point it out to him.

Hunter slammed his meaty fist down on the card table. *"Fuck. He's going to kill us."*

"Us?" I echoed, feeling a rush of anger. *"Don't you mean me? You get to soul jump into another body."*

Hunter frowned. *"I'm not sure it'll work that way. We might be in a I-go-where-you-go kind of situation."*

"Don't say that." The idea of being stuck with Hunter in life and death was horrifying.

Hunter paced around the table again. *"I should have heeded Ghost's advice. He said soul jumping would bring about my death."*

"Yeah. Why didn't you do us all a solid and listen to the man?" I closed my eyes wishing I could wake up from this nightmare within a nightmare.

"My twin isn't a man, and neither am I."

"Right," I said tiredly. We'd already covered Hunter's science-fiction origins. Those army scientists must have been really whacked out to think making a giant body snatching shifter soldier was a good idea.

Morbid curiosity had me opening my eyes and asking him, *"Were you identical twins?"*

"Carbon copies from above the waist. Below the waist Ghost is... unique."

It struck me that he was speaking of his twin in the present tense. *"I thought Dominic..."* I cleared my throat not wanting him to get fixated on Dominic again. *"... I thought all your siblings were dead."*

After sharing a mind for days, there weren't many secrets between us. I knew pretty much everything about him including the reasons behind his beef with Dominic and he knew everything about me, not that my life had been even half as exciting as his.

Hunter kicked the chair around and straddled it. *"I just found out Ghost is alive. The army is keeping him in some under-ground research facility. I should be searching for him right now, but I'm trapped here with you."* He glared at me as if I was the one who'd screwed the pooch.

I shook my head. *"You're the one trespassing, man. Why did you have to do the body snatcher thing with me, anyway? Why couldn't you have possessed somebody else... somebody like Ronnie?"* My selfish, womanizing, douchebag of a friend deserved this hell more than I did.

"You know why," Hunter said in that deep monster voice that used to terrify me.

"Because of Lee," I said with a sigh. Hunter was obsessed with the woman I loved. He believed there was some supernatural connection between them.

As if on cue Hunter exclaimed, *"She's my mate."*

I shook my head. *"She's not your mate, whatever the hell that means, and she doesn't want you."*

He smirked. *"You didn't see her riding my cock an hour ago."*

He had sex with her again. A mixture of anger and horror rushed through me. *"You were supposed to keep your hands— which are technically my hands — off her."* Back in the gym, I'd agreed to let him take over my body on the condition he not touch Lee. Unfortunately, he'd shoved me so far down into the recesses of my mind I'd had no awareness of what was going on.

Hunter's grin didn't even waver. *"My bad."*

Jesus. I scrubbed my hands down my face. *"Did you hurt her?"* If he had, I'd figure out some way to destroy him.

"I'd never hurt her, but I made her scream." Hunter flashed me his fangs. *"You should thank me. She'd never let you touch her otherwise."*

Man. I wished I could drop kick this guy out of my body, if only to stomp on his face. *"The only reason she had sex with you is because she thought you were me, asshole."*

Hunter shook his head. *"You're dreaming, cocksucker. I saw the two of you together that first night."*

Our army tent surroundings morphed into a familiar bedroom with wood-paneled walls. The cot underneath me shifted into Lee's lumpy queen bed and Gran's collection of ceramic frog's appeared on the dresser across from where I was laying. My favorite frog, the one with the pipe and top hat, wasn't there though. I wondered what happened to it.

Everything else looked just as it did the last time I'd been in here. Even Lee's closet door was ajar giving me a tanta-lizing view of the leather, lace, and spandex outfits she often wore for work.

Hunter marched over to the window and began playing peek-a-boo with the curtains. *"I watched you two from over here."*

"That's just wrong, man." I was appalled but not surprised. Nothing he did surprised me at this point. He could have told me he'd been spying on me since birth and I would have believed him. *"But if you watched us, you saw for yourself how she feels about me."*

Hunter gave a cold laugh. *"All I saw was you doing a piss-poor job of eating her out and then her ordering you from her room."*

His barb shouldn't have hurt, but it did. Having Lee reject me after we'd finally crossed the friend boundary stung. Still, I wasn't about to show Hunter he'd scored a hit. *"Lee cares for me."*

"Sure, like a brother or a gay roommate."

"Whatever, man. I made Lee come several times."

Hunter stalked over to the bed and stood over me.

Three days ago, his intimidation tactic might have worked, but now I held his inhuman glare without blinking. *"What?"*

"Understand this motherfucker, the only reason she let you touch her that night was because she was compelled to have sex. She never would have otherwise."

I sat up. *"Compelled? What do you mean by that?"*

Ignoring my question, Hunter leaned down so his huge melon of a head was in my face. *"You're not her mate. I am."*

"You don't know that."

He growled. *"I knew she was my mate the first time we were alone together."* He waved his hand and a hazy version of himself and Lee appeared in the corner of the room near the door.

The ghostly version of Lee sat across from Hunter in nothing but a G-string and stilettos. Smiling, she crooked her finger at him and beckoned him over. It wasn't one of her fake smiles either.

She does like him.

As I watched Lee proposition Hunter, I swallowed hard. *"Did you two..."*

"No," he said quickly, answering my unspoken question. *"But only because I can't mate her in my body. I'd... tear her apart."* He waved his hand and the smokey images of himself and Lee vanished. *"That's why I need your body."*

Great. I was supposed to be his sex puppet. *"It still doesn't prove your point."*

"She's my mate," he insisted again.

I had to ask the obvious question. *"Why can't she be my mate too?"*

He frowned.

Deciding to mess with the guy, I reclined back with my fingers laced together under my head. *"Maybe she's got a bunch of mates. Did you ever think of that? You, me, and Dominic."* I threw the sergeant's name out knowing it would piss Hunter off.

"No!" he roared. *"She's mine."* He took a deep breath. *"And Ghost's too."*

"Wait, what?"

"My twin and I share everything, of course we share the same mate."

"Of course," I repeated sarcastically, hoping to hell I never encountered Hunter's brother. *Jesus. What if he decides to soul jump into me too?*

Suddenly, the sharp, pungent odor of ammonia ripped us both out of the dream or whatever we were sharing. Thankfully, I ended up in the driver's seat of my body this time.

I opened my eyes and found Dominic squatting next to me with smelling salts in his hand. *Jesus. He's huge.*

"*He's not that big,*" Hunter groused from the back of my mind.

I made the mistake of moving my head and payed for it with stabbing pain. *Man, that hurts.* I probably had some kind of permanent brain damage after all the hits I'd taken the past few days.

"*This is nothing, you pussy. Try being hit with a grenade,*" Hunter taunted.

Groaning, I tried to rub my head and discovered my hands were bound behind my back.

"*Let me take over. I'll get us out of the restraints in thirty seconds flat.*" Hunter actually sounded excited about it.

"*Shut up, man. You're the reason we're in this mess.*" I didn't care how good Hunter was with restraints, I'd never willingly give him control of my body again. Not after what he just done with Lee.

As if my thoughts had conjured her, Lee appeared behind Dominic. "Reed, is that you?"

"Yeah," I couldn't help staring at her boobs. She'd knotted her shirt, well my shirt actually, under her breasts and it put all her cleavage on display. "You look amazing."

"*Fuck yeah she does,*" Hunter purred in agreement.

She gave me a weak smile that didn't reach her eyes. "Are you hearing Hunter's voice in your head right now?"

"*Does she want to talk to me?*" Hunter asked, sounding thrilled.

I sighed. "Yes. Unfortunately."

Dominic, who still crouched over me, scowled. "What's he saying, Hippie?"

"*Tell Dom I'm going to rip his lungs out of his body and—*"

"That he's going to kill you," I summarized, wiggling my fingers to get rid of the pins and needles feeling. "Can you cut me loose?" I figured he wouldn't kill me with Lee standing right there.

"Please free him," Lee pleaded. "You can see he's not a threat, sir."

Looking none too happy, Dominic pulled out one of his knives and sliced through the zip ties around my wrists and ankles.

An unmanly moan burst from my lips as blood returned to my hands and feet. I wanted to sit up, but I was afraid if I tried, I'd only lose consciousness again.

Lee stepped around Dominic and knelt next to me. "Reed we're going to get that demon out of you."

"Demon?" Hunter repeated, sounding confused.

"And then you and I are going to punish it for what it's done to you... to us." Her eyes blazed with fury.

Dominic gave her a sharp look.

Lee continued. "You can tell Hunter he's never going to touch me again."

Hunter was momentarily shocked into silence. I sensed her anger blindsided him.

Maybe it was a messed up form of Stockholm Syndrome, but I was feeling strangely defensive of the guy. "Hunter thinks he's your mate."

Lee grimaced. "He's nothing but a rapist and once we get him out of you, I'm going to cut off his monster-cock."

Dominic coughed. "I didn't agree to that."

"And I didn't agree to have sex with a stranger," Lee said, loudly into my ear. "Can he hear me?"

I nodded and immediately wished I hadn't. The throbbing pain in my head seemed to get worse.

"Fuck you, Hunter," Lee yelled.

I winced from the loud ringing in my ears and from the bewildered despair coming from Hunter.

"She can't mean that," the big guy said in a rush. *"I'm her mate. She has to understand that—"*

I interrupted him. *"No. You don't understand, man. You crossed a line. You hurt her. You hurt me."* I let him feel my disgust and anger.

"But I-I," he stammered, lost for words.

From sharing a mind with him, I knew he wasn't evil. He was amoral as hell, and one of those the-ends-justify-the-means kind of guys, but he didn't enjoy hurting people. I knew he adored Lee and that she'd become the center of his messed up world, but that didn't absolve him from what he'd done to us.

I looked up at Dominic feeling a flash of hope. "How do we get him out?"

Dominic reached over Lee and clapped one of his enormous hands on my shoulder. "We're formulating a plan."

"He has no idea," Hunter groaned. *"This is so fucked. I'm trapped in you. My mate hates me and Dom—"*

"Shut the hell up!" I had no patience for another one of Hunter's pity parties.

Dominic jerked his hand back, and I realized I'd yelled out loud.

"Sorry, that was directed at Hunter. No disrespect intended, man."

"It's, sir," Dominic corrected with a scowl.

"Fucking asshole," Hunter grumbled.

Lee cupped my face in her hands bringing my attention back to her. "Reed, we don't know how to get Hunter out just yet, but we can suppress him." She held out her hand to Dominic who was digging into a large Ziplock bag.

He filled a syringe with the contents from a small bottle. Then he placed the syringe onto her palm.

"What's that?"

"Morphine," Dominic answered peering at the bottle.

I struggled to sit up. "Jesus, isn't heroin made from that?"

"*Yes,*" Hunter growled. *"Do not inject that shit into our body."*

"For the last time, it's my body!" I mentally shouted.

Lee inspected the syringe. "Hasn't the nurse been giving you this?"

"No. Sharon's been giving me pills." I didn't mention that the nurse was almost out of them.

"You don't need pills and you don't need that shit. If you want me to be quiet, I'll become a motherfucking mute," Hunter pleaded.

"An injection should last for up to six hours." Dominic shook the bottle of clear liquid.

"I'm not even going to ask how you know that," Lee said, shaking her head. Then glancing back at me, she said, "We need you to keep taking this until we can exorcize Hunter."

"What the fuck?" shouted Hunter.

I stared at her in disbelief. "You're asking me to become a junkie?" This was the woman who didn't even like me smoking pot with Ronnie.

"Don't do it, cocksucker." Hunter was getting agitated. I sensed him surging inside me, trying to take control. *"We can't fight with that shit in our bodies. We'll be helpless and dependent on others."*

"It's only for a little while," Lee said, giving me a pleading look.

Jesus. I'd do anything for this woman and getting high for the sake of some inner peace didn't sound like the worse plan ever. "Okay." I held out my arm.

"No!" Hunter roared.

Lee lined up the tip of the needle in a vein on the inside of my elbow. There was a tiny pinprick of pain and then she was pressing the plunger.

Hunter let loose with a string of obscenities as the most incredible feeling of warmth and relaxation hit me.

Every ache and pain faded away along with Hunter's voice.

Lee hugged me to her. "It's going to be okay."

It was already okay. *So okay.* My eyes closed, and I sank into a Hunter-free euphoria where nothing mattered. Nothing...

12

LEE

"Pick up the pace, Ms. Walker," Dominic shouted from across the field.

The cold morning air seared my lungs as I tried to coax my screaming muscles to work harder.

Just one more lap.

The sharp, stabbing pain in my side was excruciating, but I didn't dare stop.

"Faster, Ms. Walker, or you'll do ten more."

God. I hate that man. If Hunter was a demon, Dominic was the devil himself. And seven days ago I'd made a freaking deal with him.

Cursing my stupidity, I lowered my head and pushed through the last lap.

Almost there.

Blood roared in my ears.

All the other members of yellow team were lined up near one of the soccer goal posts with Sergeant Pain in the Ass himself.

Eden and Nikki, a former college student whose horn-rimmed glasses were fogged this morning, gave me looks of sympathy. The other members of my team seemed confused and irritated that Dominic kept interrupting our morning training to discipline me.

In just the last hour, I'd had to run laps for not holding my knife correctly, not stabbing the zombie scarecrow in the head with enough force, and for forgetting to say, "yes, sir" about a dozen times.

All week it had been like this—Dominic nit picking the shit out of everything I did or didn't do to his satisfaction. It was especially ridiculous considering I'd put myself squarely in the middle of yellow team as far as my fighting skills. I had nowhere near the strength and physical stamina of some of the guys on the team, but at least I hadn't had to be carried to the nurse like Paula and Jerry after tackling one of Dominic's insane obstacle courses. But maybe the joke was on me, because both of them got bumped down to green team. Green team didn't have to do any of this crap.

Almost there. With a great heaving breath, I made it to the goal post. My legs promptly gave out, and I collapsed face-first into the yellowed grass.

"Lee!" Eden called out. She rushed over only to be intercepted by Dominic.

"Back in line," he ordered.

No one, other than me, was allowed to yell at my sister, but I was in no position to school Dominic on that. All I could do was lay there panting and trying not to puke my guts out. Not that I had any food to vomit. I guess it was a good thing Dominic forced us to skip breakfast this morning.

Dominic's boots crunched through the stiff grass as he approached me. He stopped a few inches from my face.

Damn. His combat boots were so shiny, I could almost see my reflection in them.

"On your feet, soldier."

I wanted to shout that I wasn't a soldier and never wanted

to become one, but my body begged me to keep my smart-ass comments to myself for once. My muscles quaked as I tried to push myself up. Halfway there, my arms buckled, and I face-planted back on the ground.

A few people in line snickered.

Crap. I used to think I was in amazing shape from pole dancing. But Dominic's trainings had shown me what a joke that was. For the past seven days he'd had us doing calisthenic exercises, weight training, weapons training, and navigating obstacle courses for hours every day. We'd all have killer bodies by the end of this, assuming we survived it.

Sucking in a deep breath, I flipped over on my back.

It was a rare cloudless day and Dominic's gorgeous face was backlit with morning sunlight as he stared down at me. His full lips were curved like a cupid's bow and those midnight eyes seemed to see straight into my soul.

It didn't seem fair that the man could be so beautiful while putting me through such torment. But then again, Lucifer had been an angel once.

"Get up, Ms. Walker," Dominic ordered again.

I lifted my hand hoping he might help me to my feet.

Instead, he turned on his heel, kicking dirt and grass into my sweat-soaked face as he walked away.

Asshole.

Eden made a sound of sympathy. It looked as if she was going to defy Dominic's orders and assist me, but I motioned for her to stay in line. No need for her to join me on Dominic's shit list. No one else made eye contact with me except for Karen, her blond daughter, Tori, and her brunette sixteen-year-old granddaughter, Kelsey. They all lifted their matching sharp-pointed noses and smiled meanly in my direction.

Bitches.

If Zara, Sai, or Dev were here, they would have offered to

help me, but they along with everyone else with a military background or survival experience had been assigned to red team. Those lucky bastards were at the top of the new civilian food chain around here.

Dominic allotted red team extra rations and first dibs on showers and patrols. They also got the nice group assignments like security and sustainability while most of us yellow team grubs were left rotating through sanitation, food-prep, and caring for the members of green team who lacked the ability to care for themselves.

Sighing, I hefted myself into a wobbly standing position which seemed to pacify Dominic for the moment.

"Attention," he yelled.

At once, everyone sucked in their stomachs and stood upright.

I hurried into the end of the line and did my best to lift my chin, put my shoulders back and stick out my chest. *Damn.* That stitch in my side still hurt. I had to take short, shallow breaths around the searing pain.

Dominic marched up and down our line with his hands clasped behind his back. "None of you have mastered the skills you will need to pass your field training test."

Field training test? I glanced around glad to see I wasn't the only one wearing a confused expression.

Enrique, the buff, thirty-something personal trainer Dominic had made our team leader raised his hand.

Dominic nodded in his direction. "Mr. Martinez, do you have a question?"

"Yes, sir. Can you explain the field training test, sir?"

I would have rolled my eyes at Enrique's ass kissing, but he was too much of a nice guy. Besides his husband, Roger, who was prematurely grey at thirty-five, was standing right next to me in line. Roger was a psychologist who'd gone out of his way to spend time with Reed this past week. For that reason alone, I'd never disrespect either man.

Dominic gave a half-smile that was anything but warm. "Starting next week, I will bring all members of red team and yellow team into town to confront the infected. Those that defeat the enemy, pass their test."

"W-what happens if we don't defeat them?" Nikki asked in a wavering voice.

Dominic gave her a hard look. "Then you die. If, in the unlikely scenario, you somehow survive your encounter with the dead, but cannot defeat them, you'll be exiled."

Shit. Just when I thought putting up with all Dominic's stupid orders and punishments wasn't enough. Now I'd have to fight for my life against Biters or risk being thrown out. *And if I'm exiled will our bargain still be valid, or will Dominic be free to kill Reed?*

My blood chilled.

The frantic murmurs of the others told me I wasn't the only one freaking out at this news.

Dominic raised his fist, and everyone went silent. "Today's training exercise should further your odds of success. Wait here." He marched around the side of the school, leaving us in the middle of the field.

The moment he was out of sight, I gave into the throbbing pain in my side and doubled over.

A thin arm wrapped around my waist, steadying me. "I've got you, sissy."

I gave Eden a grateful look. "That's supposed to be my line."

She laughed softly.

I'd missed her. The past week we had spent little time together. Dominic didn't let us talk during his trainings and bedtime didn't really count because as soon as lights went out in the classroom, we all passed the hell out. Dominic's trainings were definitely the cure for insomnia.

As I leaned against her, the tactical ax Eden had holstered around her waist dug into my side. I adjusted her melee weapon and said, "They're keeping you pretty busy in medical, huh?"

Eden's background as a vet assistant had been enough to place her on the medical team with Isaac, an EMT, Olivia, who'd been in nursing school, and of course Sharon the nurse. My former serving gig had earned me a place on the food preparation team which, honestly, wasn't a terrible assignment.

She nodded. "Yeah, Sharon's been giving me a crash course in nursing 101."

"Those are some good skills to have." I took a couple deep breaths, each one coming easier than the last.

Eden dropped her arm and stepped away. "Yeah. I'd enjoy it more if Sharon wasn't still holding a grudge about the missing pain meds. I know she suspects I took them."

The accusatory look she gave me had me glancing down at my sneakers. "They're serving a good purpose."

"How can you say that? Have you seen Reed lately? He's a mess."

I swallowed hard unable to argue with her. At least Dominic allowed Reed to stay by himself in the music room where his descent into drug addiction was mostly hidden from everyone. Although not Eden apparently.

"How could you give him those drugs?" Eden searched my face as if trying to find a reasonable explanation.

I had none to give her. Dominic made me swear to tell no one about Hunter. The sergeant's many attempts to draw Hunter out of Reed had met with zero success. I was beginning to think we needed another plan. Reed's health and state of mind were deteriorating too rapidly.

I straightened, finding that the pain in my side had subsided. "You'll just have to trust me."

Eden let out a harsh laugh. "I'm just supposed to trust you when you never trust me."

I stepped away so I could give her my big sister glare. "If you're so trustworthy, tell me where you've been sneaking off to in the middle of the night."

Zara had filled me in on Eden's hour-long bathroom breaks while we all slept. I had a hunch Eden was sneaking off to meet up with Mike.

"I have an overactive bladder," Eden said too quickly.

"No, you don't. Stop lying."

Eden's expression turned cagey. "Stop being so overbearing—" she caught sight of something over my shoulder and paled.

I spun around and my stomach dropped. Close to twenty Biters lurched around the side of the school. They were headed straight toward us. "Oh, shit!"

"Where's Dominic?" The sergeant was nowhere in sight.

The horde must have crashed through the front gate.

Several members of yellow team screamed.

"Zombies!"

"Run!"

Heart pounding, I grabbed Eden's hand. "Hurry we have to get back inside."

Most of our team had the same idea. We all rushed to the gym door.

Mario got there first. "It's locked," he shouted, banging his tattooed fist on the outside of the door.

Clang.

Grady hit the door with his crowbar just missing Mario's head.

"Watch it, *ese*," Mario snarled at him.

The moans of the dead grew in volume.

I glanced up to see the Biters were only ten yards away. They blocked off our path to the playground and the front of the school.

"Why aren't they opening the door?" wailed Nikki.

"Because this is part of Sarge's training," Enrique said slowly.

Mario cursed in Spanish. "It's Christmas Eve. What kind of sick fucker unleashes a bunch of zombies on Christmas eve?"

"Look, none of the Biters have arms," Grady called out.

He's right. Every single one of the dead, from the elderly man dragging an oxygen tank behind him to the small child tottering after the rest of the herd was missing their arms.

"They don't have teeth either," added Roger.

Now that he mentioned it, the Biters weren't making that awful clicking sound even though their mouths were opening and closing.

It didn't matter though. Even armless and toothless, they were a threat, and I had to keep Eden safe.

"Come on!" Leaving the others to fend for themselves, I dragged Eden toward the storage shed. Maybe we could hole up inside.

Eden struggled when she saw the direction we were headed. "No, not the shed. How about there?" She pointed at a large tree growing near the back fence. "We can climb it."

"Good thinking." Not only would it get us out of reach of the zombies, we could use it to climb over the twelve-foot wrought-iron fence and escape into the empty back alley.

We quickly switched directions and hoofed it sixty yards to the thirty-foot tall Mesquite.

By the time we got there, my legs were shaking, and that damn stitch was throbbing under my ribs again. Ignoring the pain, I pushed Eden up and climbed the tree after her. We'd only made it a dozen feet before the limbs became too thin to support our weight. At least we were high enough off the ground to be out of danger and we had a bird's-eye view of the shit show happening below.

Members of our team had scattered. Some, like Karen and her family, were running all over the field screaming for help. Some, like Enrique and Roger, were grouped up near one of the soccer goal posts trying to fend off the dead. And the rest were still beating frantically on the door to the gym. Mario and Grady protected them by whacking off the advancing dead—Grady with his crowbar and Mario with his machete. Together the men put down at least twelve of the Biters.

Despite my dislike of Rosie's dad, I had to admit he fought well. After Grady and Mario took out the Biters attacking their group, the two men rushed to assist Enrique and Roger holding off the zombies by the goal post. Seeing the four men putting down Biter after Biter seemed to give the other members of yellow team confidence. Soon everyone was fighting back.

Even Karen put the child Biter out of its misery with her gardening hoe.

Eden started climbing down from the tree.

I grabbed her arm to stop her. "What are you doing?"

"Going to help them," she answered.

I tightened my grip. "No. Stay here. They can take care of themselves."

The sound of a slow clap had us both glancing down.

Dominic stood at the base of the tree. "Bravo, Ms. Walker. That attitude will get you and everyone else killed."

Crap.

Eden gave me a withering look and jumped down. "I'm sorry, sir. I'd like to assist my team, sir."

Dominic nodded and waved her on.

Eden pulled out her ax and ran toward the middle of the field.

"Eden!" Terrified she'd get hurt I jumped out of the tree after her.

Dominic seized my arm, anchoring me in place. "Let her go."

"No." I tried to wrench away. "I have to protect her."

"She doesn't need your protection. Look." Dominic pointed at the field where Eden joined the others beating down the last remaining Biter.

"Yes, she does." *What if she has a scratch or an open wound and some zombie blood gets in it?* I thrashed against Dominic trying to get him to release me.

He only tightened his bruising grip.

A loud cheer went up. Eden and the other yellow team members danced around the dismembered Biters waving their weapons in the air.

Some tension left me, and I sagged against Dominic.

He thrust me away from him so quickly I stumbled. "Your team has defeated the enemy, no thanks to your cowardice."

I lifted my chin. "I'm not a coward, but I have to keep my sister safe."

His expression could have been carved from stone. "We fight together, or we fall together."

I bared my teeth. "She and Reed are the only things that matter. I would kill for them. I will die for them. Oh, why am I telling you this? You don't understand. You've probably never loved anything in your life."

His glare turned my blood to ice. "Your love makes them weak." He raised his voice and shouted, "Congratulations yellow team, you've passed this training exercise. Go inside and enjoy breakfast."

As if waiting on cue, the door to the gym swung open and Avi, who'd somehow earned his place among Dominic's squad of soldiers, beckoned everyone inside.

I started for the door only to have Dominic snag my

elbow again. "They passed, you failed, Ms. Walker. As punishment, you'll clean up the entire field. Bury the infected next to the shed."

"B-but there's like twenty zombies." I turned my gaze to the body parts strewn everywhere. It'd take me all day to pick them up and bury them by myself.

"You will stay out here until the task is completed."

Great. Just freaking great. I watched Eden follow the rest of the team through the gym door and sighed. "Yes, sir."

His top lip curled a fraction of an inch before the evil son of a bitch walked away, leaving me to my gruesome punishment.

Ah, hell. He really is the devil.

13

LEE

The sun moved all the way across the sky in the time it took me to drag all the bodies to the shed and start digging. The ground was soft and wet due to the rain but shoveling a mass grave deep enough for all the dismembered corpses was harder than I'd imagined.

It didn't help that I was exhausted and trembling with thirst. I'd even started hallucinating. Just an hour ago, I'd heard a soft whimpering sound coming from somewhere nearby. I'd checked through my pile of bodies twice just to be sure it wasn't coming from them. But the Biters were all dead in the never-getting-up again way. Finally, I'd realized the noise was most likely coming from my delirious mind which probably meant my extreme thirst had moved into severe dehydration.

My body needed water desperately, but I was too stubborn to ask Sergeant Pain in the Ass for a drink. I'd rather die of dehydration than beg for his mercy. Maybe he'd feel bad when he found my lifeless husk out here.

Cursing Dominic, I stabbed the shovel into the dirt, but

when I tried to lift it out my arms shook so badly, the shovel tipped to the side and the dirt fell back in.

Dammit. I sat back on the edge of the pitiful hole feeling lower than I had in a really long time. Every single muscle in my body ached, I was covered in zombie blood, and I was smellier than Vincent. Even worse, I'd broken every single one of my nails and the palm of my right hand was covered in angry blisters. I rested my head against the shovel handle and fought the urge to cry.

No. I won't give Dominic the satisfaction. I'd be damned if I'd ever let that man see me cry.

Speaking of the devil... The sound of footsteps had me snapping my eyes open, but it wasn't Dominic approaching.

Avi, looking dangerous and surprisingly sexy in a black long-sleeve T-shirt and low-slung jeans, strode over to me. "Sarge sent me to see what's taking you so long."

"Of course he did." Because I needed another judgmental asshole in my life right now. "Fuck off, Avi." Normally, I'd be cordial to Zara's older brother even though he still treated me as if I was some kind of threat to his family. But I was so out of cordial. If he got too close, I might just whack him over the head with the shovel and add him to my pile.

"Do you always bite the hand that feeds you?" Avi waved a water bottle at me.

I dropped the shovel and forced a fake smile. "It's good to see you Mr. Sighn. Can I please have that?"

Giving me a sour look, he twisted open the top and handed me the bottle. Letting out an eager cry, I slammed it down like a frat boy at a keg party. Water dribbled down my chin and I started to wipe it away. Thank God I caught myself in time. My hands were disgusting.

Avi looked between the pile of bodies and my shallow hole. "You must have really pissed off Sarge. What did you do?"

I stared into the empty water bottle wishing it would magically refill. "I saved my sister's ass instead of putting the T in teamwork."

Avi pursed his lips but said nothing.

Whatever. I didn't need his judgement too. "Family first," I muttered. It'd been one of my Gran's favorite sayings. Of course, Gran had considered every living soul her family, whereas, I only had two names on that list. One was an ungrateful brat and the other I'd forced to become a drug addict. My shoulders slumped and my mood darkened even further.

Avi stared at me as if he were seeing me for the first time. "I agree."

"Really?" Now that I thought about it, he looked after his siblings the way I looked after Eden and Reed, so maybe we had more in common than I thought.

Avi nodded. "I'd sacrifice everyone in the safe house to save my brothers and sister." His unflinching stare made it clear I'd definitely be one of the first to die.

Right back at you, buddy. "Well, don't let Dominic hear you say that, or you'll join me digging holes."

Deciding I'd had enough of a break, I stood and bent over to pick up the shovel.

Avi reached around me and grabbed the handle. When I tried to take it from him, he not so gently shoved me back on my ass.

"What are you doing?"

"Something I'm going to regret." He started digging.

I watched him shovel my hole for twenty minutes before saying, "You're probably not supposed to be helping me."

"No," he grimaced. "But here I am anyway."

"Thank you," I said, feeling a rush of gratitude.

"I don't require your thanks." He used the bottom of his

shirt to wipe the sweat on his brow and flashed me washboard abs and an Adonis belt that made my mouth dry.

Holy hell. Avi was ripped. Like plaster him on the cover of a romance novel kind of ripped. I realized in that moment what a damn fine-looking man he was with his muscular body, swarthy skin, and hazel eyes. It was easy to overlook him when Dominic, Sai, and Reed were standing around in their masculine perfection, but he was as hot as they were in his own understated way.

All at once my gratitude shifted into something else entirely. I suddenly wished I didn't look and smell like the inside of a cemetery dumpster. I glanced down at myself noticing a glob of intestine stuck to my elbow. Shuddering, I flicked it away.

"You shouldn't antagonize Sarge," Avi said, returning to his back-breaking work. "Men like him need to feel in control. Give him that control."

I scoffed. "Never."

Avi shook his head. "You're as stubborn as my sister, but even Zara knows when to submit to authority."

I stood up. "I'll never submit to Dominic or anyone else."

He frowned. "Haven't you heard the story of the willow and the oak?"

"No, but I have a feeling I'm about to."

He ignored my sarcasm. "One day, an arrogant oak tree taunted the willow tree by claiming it was the strongest tree in the forest. The next day a hurricane hit. The willow bent and survived the forceful winds. But the inflexible oak tree refused to give way and was torn out by the roots. Do you see the moral of the story?"

"Yeah, better to die as a mighty oak than live as a weak willow tree."

Avi sighed and shook his head.

Having had enough of his lecture, I held out my hand. "Give me back the shovel, willow tree."

"No."

I set my jaw. "It's my punishment. Let me finish it."

Avi grabbed my right wrist and shoved my palm up toward my face. "Don't be stupid. You've got Biter blood and blisters all over your hand. What happens when those blisters crack open?"

Oh, God. I'll become infected. I sat back down, staring at the small line of fluid-pockets along the heel of my hand. I was tempted to wipe away some dirt and zombie goo caked around the blisters, but I didn't want to risk popping them.

Crap. Avi might have saved my life.

Seeming happy with the depth of the hole, Avi turned his attention to the bodies. Feeling a bit dazed, I watched him toss them in one by one. I had to look away when he got to the body of the child. There was something about seeing that small face that drove home the magnitude of the apocalypse.

That little life had been snuffed out far too early. He'd never grow up. He'd never go to school. He'd never play ball in this school yard. It was so damn unfair.

Grief settled heavy in my chest as Avi covered the grave with dirt.

He patted the top of the mound with the shovel, dropped the tool, and looked over at me. "It's done. Let's head back inside."

I tried to stand, but a massive leg cramp drove me back down to the ground.

"I've got you." Avi strode over, scooped me up like I weighed nothing, and carried me to the gym door.

I should have insisted on walking, but I was so damn tired and his woodsy, masculine scent warmed my insides.

He balanced my weight in one hand so he could open the door with his other.

He's strong. A vision of what he could do with that strength made my heart beat faster.

Seeming to mistake my shallow breathing, Avi said, "You can relax. Sarge isn't here."

Dominic wasn't the only one missing. The gym was deserted. "Where is everyone?"

"The cafeteria. Can't you smell dinner?"

Now that he mentioned it, the air did smell amazing. My stomach rumbled as I caught a whiff of turkey. "It's the Christmas Eve dinner," I said more to myself than him.

Paula, the former baker in charge of my assigned group, had gotten Dominic's permission to prepare a big feast for Christmas Eve dinner. We'd been peeling potatoes for days. No doubt she'd be pissed at me for not being there to help. Which meant I'd be on dish washing duty for the rest of the week. Wincing, I glanced down at my destroyed hands.

Avi strode across the basketball court. "As a morale booster, Sarge is allowing all civilians to celebrate tonight. He pushed lights out to midnight and lifted the ban on alcohol."

"How generous of him," I said dryly.

He frowned as if he disapproved of my reaction. "You should clean up."

I couldn't even take offense at his comment, that's how bad I smelled.

He set me down by the girl's locker room door. "Make sure you take care of that hand."

"I will. Thank you for helping me," I said, forcing my muscles to bear my weight.

"Don't mention it. Like seriously, don't mention it to anyone, especially Sarge."

"I'll take it to the grave," I promised.

He smiled and flashed me a pair of the sexiest dimples I'd ever seen.

Wow. I felt dizzy for a second and it had nothing to do with being tired and hungry.

I must have swayed a bit because he put his hand on my shoulder to steady me. "Are you okay?"

Hell no. I was totally lusting after my friend's brother. And not the sexy brother or the sweet brother—the asshole brother. Maybe I had a type after all. *Assholes.*

When I realized he was staring at me waiting for a response, I forced a smile. "I'll see you later, willow tree." Hopefully, a lot later when I'd come to my freaking senses.

He nodded and walked over to the boy's locker room probably to clean my stink off him. I didn't let go of my breath until he'd disappeared inside.

A strange feeling swirled around my stomach. It took me a second to place it. Anticipation. I was actually looking forward to seeing Avi again which was completely idiotic because we lived together, so of course I'd see him again.

Exhaustion must be getting to me. I pushed inside the locker room, vowing to forget all about Zara's least favorite brother.

Thankfully, there was no one inside to yell at me for using more than my daily allocation of rainwater. After cleaning my hand and gulping down handfuls of water, I stripped and used the rest of the bucket along with half a bottle of shampoo to clean my entire body. Then I went in search for something to wear in the piles of recently hand-washed laundry.

Dominic had mandated a communal clothing system which made for some interesting options. I decided on Kelsey's leopard print leggings that I paired with one of Zara's skin-tight midriff baring black shirts. Since I wasn't able to find any clean underwear that fit, I went commando. However, I found fingerless black gloves that covered my blisters and a pair of black platform heels that were only half a size too small.

The outfit was more appropriate for a rock concert than

the apocalypse, but beggars couldn't be choosers. Besides, the form-fitting clothes made me look good. And I wanted to look good, both to show Sergeant Pain in the Ass that his punishment hadn't affected me and to show Avi that I cleaned up well.

After brushing my damp hair until it fell in a dark waterfall down my back, I fixed my broken nails with an emery board I found in one locker, and I slapped on some makeup from the case I found sitting near the sink. Although the fading light through the window made it hard to see in the mirror, I was satisfied with what I could make out of my reflection.

Just wait until Dominic and Avi see me.

I slid my knife into my waistband and turned to leave. Before I got to the door, I pinched my nipples through my shirt for good luck. It was something Cami had started during my early days at the club. My throat tightened for a moment as I thought of her. If Cami were here, she'd slap my ass and tell me to go show Dominic he'd never break me. She'd probably also tell me to fuck Avi's brains out. *Hell.* She'd probably tell me to fuck Dominic's brains out too.

The sudden image of me riding a naked Dominic while sucking Avi's cock took my breath away. I shook my head rejecting the ridiculous fantasy. *What's wrong with me?* I already had a guy. Sure, Reed was possessed by a demon and lost in a fog of drug addiction, but wasn't I supposed to be true to him? The answer should have been clear, but it wasn't. I kept returning to Zara's view on relationships. Maybe having multiple lovers was the key to happiness.

My stomach rumbled. Pushing thoughts of men from my mind, I left the locker room. Rehydrating had eased nearly all my aches and pains allowing me to stride through the gym and out into the empty hallway without limping. The sound of muffled laughter and mouthwatering scents drew me to the open cafeteria door down the hall.

It seemed as if every member of red, yellow, and green team was crammed inside. Most people sat with their families at one of the many tables running the length of the room, but some stood making small talk near the buffet tables in the back as if they were at some office Christmas party.

Adding to the holiday ambiance was the decorated nine-foot Christmas tree set up in the far corner of the room. The sight of it would have been heartwarming if I didn't hate Christmas trees. They always brought back memories of another tree—one that was decorated in the blood of my mother and older sister.

The cheerful chatter suddenly seemed too loud and overwhelming. Deciding I really wasn't that hungry, I turned to leave.

A heavily muscled chest stopped me in my tracks.

❧ 14 ❧

LEE

Avi grunted.

"Sorry," I murmured, relieved that I'd face-planted into his muscular chest and not Dominic's.

My breath went a little jagged as I noticed he'd cleaned up too. Although he was still rocking his signature five o'clock shadow much to my delight, his head was freshly shaved, and his skin was damp. He'd also changed into a clean pair of jeans and a navy T-shirt that carried the scent of his woodsy cologne.

His eyes widened as he stared down at me.

Feeling attractive for the first time in forever, I gave him my most seductive smile.

He frowned. "You went a little too heavy-handed with the makeup, don't you think?"

My smile dimmed.

"And what are you wearing on your feet? Those are completely inappropriate. Can you outrun a zombie in those?"

Why did I ever think this guy was sexy? "Fuck off, willow tree." Needing to get away from him before I did something

I'd regret, like kick him in the shins with my totally inappropriate heels, I marched into the cafeteria.

Nearly every guy in the room stopped what they were doing and stared in my direction.

Now that's what I'm going for. My confidence returned with a vengeance, which was good because all those guys' wives and girlfriends were now glaring at me with barely veiled contempt.

Whatever. Let them hate. I'd drink their envy like Kool-Aid tonight.

Seemingly irritated, Avi walked up behind me. "You're supposed to put all your weapons down there." He pointed at a card table I'd somehow overlooked outside the cafeteria door. The table practically bowed under the weight of the knives, guns, and other weapons lying on it. Without waiting for my permission, he pulled my knife from my waistband and walked it over to the table.

"Give that back," I demanded as he set my knife down.

"Rules are rules." He strode back and grabbed my arm. "Sarge is allowing alcohol consumption in this room only and he doesn't want any accidents."

I felt naked without my weapon. "If anyone steals my blade, I'll blame you."

"No one will take it. Look, they're sitting over there." He pointed at a table near the back wall where Eden and Reed were sitting with Zara and her non-asshole brothers.

I shook Avi's hand off my arm. He didn't have the right to touch me after insulting my outfit and taking my knife.

Avi's lips thinned, but I could give a shit. Deciding to put as much space between us as possible, I sashayed across the cafeteria as quickly as I could in the platform heels.

Ed, the youngest and best looking of the Richardson brothers, stood at his family's table.

"Excuse me," I said to the stocky guy, trying to get

around him.

Ed's square jaw dropped, and his pale blue eyes moved up and down my body. "Hey, beautiful. Can I get you a drink?" He offered me the plastic cup in his hand.

"No," Avi answered, knocking Ed's drink away.

Beer sloshed over the side of the cup and onto the face of the blond woman seated at the table.

I had to laugh when I saw it was Karen.

The salty bitch squealed and stared daggers at me because it was all my fault, apparently.

Feeling slightly better about life, I maneuvered around Ed and strode over to my family's table. I slid into the empty seat between Eden and Reed. "Hi, guys."

Eden gave me a sour look and Reed's vacant expression didn't change.

"Lee!" Zara exclaimed, looking up from the poker game she had going with Sai and Dev. "You look hotter than the hinges of hell."

Sai stared at me, his beautiful hazel eyes nearly popping out of his head. "Well, tonight just got a thousand times better." He threw down his cards, reached across the table, and grabbed my right hand. "I hope you know CPR, because you just took my breath away."

Zara rolled her eyes. "Fruitcake is sitting right there."

Sai didn't even glance at Reed. "Say you'll spend tonight with me, darling." He squeezed my hand.

I winced as his fingers pressed the fabric of my glove against the blisters.

Avi whacked his brother on the back of the head. "She's injured. You're hurting her."

Sai dropped my hand. "Sorry."

"Get her some food," Avi ordered.

"Are you hungry?" Sai asked.

I nodded, feeling some of my appetite return.

"I'll be right back with a plate," Sai stood.

"And a drink for her too," Avi said gruffly, taking his brother's seat across from me.

Sai flipped off Avi behind his head.

I couldn't help giggling.

"I saw that," Avi said, even though he hadn't turned around. He frowned at me. "Don't encourage him."

Ugh. Avi was such a buzz kill. I couldn't believe I found him attractive for even a second.

Deciding to ignore him for the rest of the night, I turned my attention to Reed. He stared sightlessly down at the food on his paper plate.

"How are you doing, honey?"

Seeming not to hear me, Reed picked at one of the many new scabs on his forearm.

"Why don't you have some food?" I grabbed the plastic fork near his plate and pushed it into his hand. He needed to eat. In the last week, he'd dropped at least ten pounds.

His blue eyes were dull as he lifted the utensil and dug the prongs into his arm.

Oh, God. "Don't do that."

"It itches," he explained tonelessly.

"Do you want more lotion?" I'd raided the locker room to find something that would help. But not even the anti-itch creams seem to do anything for him.

"Lotion won't help. He needs to stop using," Avi said, from across the table.

Dammit. I'd been hoping no one would notice his condition. That's why Reed stayed in the music room except for meals.

Maybe he should eat his meals there too.

Guilt washed over me as I stared at Reed's gaunt face. *No.* The isolation wasn't good for him. *Hell.* None of this was good for him.

My throat tightened with despair. Dominic and I needed to figure out another way to suppress Hunter. And soon.

Dev, who sat between Avi and Zara looked up from his cards. "Would Fruitcake mind if I had some of his potatoes?"

"Stop calling him that," I snapped.

"You can have my entire dinner." Eden pushed her food across the table at Dev. "I didn't want any of this, but Paula insisted."

I intercepted her plate and shoved it back in front of her. "Eat your food, Edie." Because of Dominic's rationing, we only ate twice a day. Once in the morning and once at night. There were no other snacks allowed and I would not let her go hungry.

Eden glared daggers at me. "I'm not eating that." She jabbed her finger at the generous helping of turkey, gravy covered potatoes, and green bean and bacon casserole. "It's disgusting."

It was a freaking feast after the meager rations we'd been eating.

Avi opened his mouth as if to chastise her, but I gave him a hard look. Eden was mine to deal with.

"Eat it," I ordered. "We can't afford to waste our supplies." Being in the food prep group, I was all too aware of how little rations remained. I'd heard Dominic was going to send out scavenging parties soon, but who knew how that would go.

"I'll die before eating food that comes from animals," Eden hissed.

I took a deep breath fighting the urge to shove her face into the food.

Giving me a look of challenge, Eden shoved the plate back over to Dev. "Take it."

Avi sat back in his seat no doubt judging my response.

Screw him and screw the brat. If Eden wanted to starve, she could starve.

Dev's hand hovered over the food, his gaze bouncing between Eden and me. "I don't want to—"

"Please." I waved my hand in permission. "Someone might as well enjoy it."

Dev pushed back his glasses and grinned. Then he eagerly dove into the food.

Avi shook his head disapprovingly, and I felt as if I'd once again failed a test. He stood. "My patrol starts in five." He gave us all a hard look and said, "Behave." Then he stalked off.

Good riddance.

Eden jumped to her feet. "I've got to check on the animals."

Zara looked up from shuffling cards. "But you just checked them an hour ago."

"I-I forgot to feed the rabbits," Eden stuttered. She was such a bad liar.

"We have rabbits?" Dev asked through a mouthful of potatoes.

"Yes, and they need their dinner." Eden brushed a few breadcrumbs off her shirt. At least she'd eaten something. "I also should clean the cat boxes. It'll take a while. Lee, can you keep an eye on Rosie if Grady drops her off early tonight?"

I nodded, glancing over at the table where the little girl sat with her dad. Rosie looked miserable. Her grass-green eyes met mine as her very drunk father swayed in the seat next to her.

Feeling bad for the little girl, I waved at her. "I can't believe Grady is already shit-faced."

"And we're going to join him," Zara announced, pulling an open bottle of rum out from under the table.

"Zara!" I exclaimed in surprise. "Where did you get that?"

"If I told you, I'd have to kill you," she winked. She gave

Eden a stern look. "Your sister won't be available for babysitting tonight. Ask Olivia." She jabbed her finger at the single mom who was feeding spoonfuls of potatoes to her toddler, Sam.

Eden frowned. "But—"

Zara made a tsking sound. "It's Christmas Eve. Lee deserves to have some fun while you play hide the sausage with your soldier boy."

Eden's face flamed. "I-I—"

"I don't feel so good," a small voice said from behind her.

We all turned to look at Rosie who must have taken my wave as an invitation to join us. The little girl's face was flushed and sweat dotted her forehead.

"What's wrong?" Eden asked, kneeling down next to her.

"My head feels funny and my tummy hurts." Rosie rubbed her stomach.

Eden put her hand on the girl's forehead. "You feel warm." She looked back at us. "I'm going to take her to the nurse."

"I'll take her," I offered, standing.

Eden shook her head. "No, it's okay. You haven't eaten yet."

Before I could point out that neither had she, my sister grabbed Rosie's hand and the two of them walked away.

"I hope it's nothing serious," I said to Reed as I sat back down.

He didn't answer.

I turned to find him slumped over the table with his eyes closed. At least he hadn't fallen into his food.

Sighing, I pulled his plate in front of me. Since he obviously wouldn't eat any of it, I pinched a piece of turkey and popped it into my mouth. It was delicious. My stomach cramped demanding more. I grabbed Eden's abandoned fork and began shoveling the food into my mouth.

"I guess you took matters into your own hands," Sai said,

setting an overflowing plate down next to the one I'd nearly licked clean.

"Thanks," I said, wondering how I'd eat that much food. My hunger pains had eased completely, and I actually felt sated for the first time in over a week.

"And here's your drink." Sai gave me an apologetic look as he handed me a plastic cup, half-filled with apple juice. "Unfortunately, the beer and wine are gone. "

"I've got her covered." Zara grabbed the cup and filled it to the brim with rum.

I shook my head. "I'm not drinking that." The last time I drank alcohol I lost my virginity to a demon, and the world went to hell.

"Drink it. We can't afford to waste our supplies," she deadpanned, in a perfect imitation of my voice.

Giving her the finger, I took a swallow. The drink was surprisingly good. So good in fact, that I finished it and even let them refill my cup. Soon the room was spinning, and I was having a hard time sitting upright.

Thank goodness for Sai who'd taken Eden's seat next to me. He'd slung his arm around my waist, keeping me in place.

As the night progressed, his rock star stories had gotten funnier and the card games had gotten more challenging to follow.

"Hit me," I said to Zara when it was my turn at blackjack.

Sai chuckled. "You've got two jacks, you should stand, darling."

"Mind your own beeswax, rock star." I tapped one of his dimples deciding that he was much hotter, and much more charming than his older brother. Even so, I couldn't stop wondering if Avi would return after his patrol shift.

Zara threw down an ace.

"Blackjack, baby!" I shouted.

Zara and Sai broke out in cheers while I acted as if my win

had been anything more than dumb luck.

"Keep it down," Dev said, glancing at the empty tables around us. Nearly everyone had turned in for the night.

Zara scoffed at her youngest brother. "There's only like ten other people in here. Most are red team, and most are drunker than we are."

She was right. Grady and the Richardson brothers were singing off-key sea shanties to Karen who waved her wine bottle in the air like a drunk orchestra conductor.

Evan Dickerson, a former parkour instructor, looked as if he was about to get it on with Janelle Fremeldt. She was a stunt woman and the only female in the school with more muscles than Darcy. Both were flushed and practically sitting in each other's laps.

At the table behind them, Ben and Eric Miller, both former firefighters, were smashing back shots with Lew Cho who'd run a popular martial arts studio near the university. As if feeling my gaze, all three men looked over, their eyes glinting with interest.

Sai tightened his arm around me, clearly staking his claim.

"It's getting late." Dev tapped the watch on his wrist. "I'm going to bed."

"Aw! Don't go," his sister pleaded.

"Are you mad because we won't let you drink?" Sai asked. "You know Avi would kick our asses if we did."

Dev yawned. "I'm just tired."

His yawn was contagious and after giving in to a jaw-splitting one of my own, a wave of bone-deep exhaustion hit me.

I shrugged off Sai's arm. "I think I'm going to go to bed myself."

Sai leaned over and whispered in my ear, "Can I join you, darling?" His warm breath made goosebumps run down my neck and the smell of his bay rum cologne made my head spin.

My God. He was gorgeous. But even tipsy, I knew getting with him was a bad idea. "That's not happening, rock star."

"Give me one good reason." Sai flashed me his sexy dimples and my resolve wavered.

I glanced down at Reed. "My reason is sleeping right there."

Sai pouted. "You need more than one lover."

"That's what I told her," Zara said, taking the last swig from the rum bottle.

"Even I know that," Dev added, his eyes on the door.

It was such an odd concept. I had to know more. "What about your mother and father? Surely they were monogamous."

"We don't have a father," Dev said. "Well... other than Avi."

I blinked in surprise. "Avi's your dad?"

Sai shook his head. "We were all fathered by different men..." He gestured around at his siblings. "...not that we ever knew them."

"Did that bother you?" I asked even though I wished to hell I'd never known my own father.

Zara shrugged. "Not really. Avi was so much older than us, he practically raised us." Seeming to anticipate my next question, she added, "Our mom was always being deployed or going on reconnaissance missions, so she wasn't around a lot."

I wanted to ask more questions, but the sounds of screaming outside the room tore my attention away. "What's happening?"

The Millers and Richardsons all jumped to their feet as Enrique flew into the cafeteria and slammed the door behind him.

The yellow team leader was hyperventilating and covered with blood. "Biters! There are Biters inside the school."

LEE

The sound of gunshots going off in the hallway sobered me faster than an ice bath.

Bruce, the eldest Richardson strode over to Enrique, his barrel chest puffed out. "Is this some kind of joke?"

More shots rang out.

Someone shrieked as they ran by the door.

Terror climbed its way down my spine.

Enrique shoved Bruce away. "I need to find Roger, is Roger here?" His frantic, wild-eyed gaze landed on me. "Lee, have you seen Roger?"

"No." The last time I'd noticed Enrique's husband, he'd been eating dinner with Enrique. That had been hours ago.

"I have to find him," Enrique cried, fear thick in his voice. He turned and reached for the door handle.

"Stop. Tell us what's going on," shouted Bruce as he tried to grab the younger man.

But he was too late. Enrique pushed the door open and stepped into a crowd of people.

No. Not people.

Dozens of pale-faced zombies that immediately seized Enrique with clawing hands and snapping teeth.

Oh, God! My breath strangled in my throat. I opened and closed my eyes. *This can't be happening.*

Enrique screamed and tried to fight them off. They piled on top of him as if he was a quarterback with a football.

Bruce slammed the door on Enrique's blood-curdling shrieks.

Karen wailed hysterically.

"We have to help him," I shouted over her cries. I started toward the door, but Sai grabbed my arm.

"He can't be helped." Gone were Sai's hooded eyes and flirtatious smile. His demeanor and that of his siblings had shifted dramatically. They stood together scanning the room with an almost predatory alertness.

"We need our weapons," Dev said in a rush of breath.

Sai reached for his war hammer at the same time I fumbled for my knife.

We both came up empty.

"They're on the table outside." Zara pointed at the shaking door.

Oh, hell.

"Help," Bruce yelled, flattening his back against the wood frame. It shuddered under the beating fists of the dead.

The narrow glass pane in the door shattered. With a cry, the flinty-eyed man ducked away from the grasping hands that shot through the opening.

Karen's wails grew in volume. They seemed to be riling up the Biters.

The door frame splintered.

"We need to barricade it." Bruce grabbed the end of a table. His brothers and Grady rushed over to help him shove it against the fracturing wood.

The other door on the far side of the room shook.

"We've got it," Eric shouted as he, his brother, Evan, and Janelle began shoving tables in front of that door.

Karen's cries grew more high-pitched, and she clutched the wine bottle to her chest as if it were her lifeline.

"We need to get out of here," Sai announced in a hoarse voice as he, Zara, and Dev formed a defensive circle around me.

"No shit, Sherlock," Zara snapped, her hazel eyes scanning the windowless room.

"That door leads to the kitchen!" I exclaimed, pointing to the back of the room where the dinner buffet had been set up. "We can get outside from there." There were windows in the kitchen along with a door that led to a different, hopefully Biter-free, hallway.

"On it," Zara said, running for the kitchen door.

Dev took off after her.

"Come on," Sai tugged my arm, but I was looking down at Reed still passed out on the table.

"Help me with him," I pleaded.

Sai made a sound of frustration but dropped my elbow. Throwing his arm around Reed, he hefted the taller man up.

Reed's eyelids cracked open. "W-what's going on?"

"Biters," I said over Karen's cries.

Reed blinked, his gaze bleary as he took in the red team members trying to barricade the doors. "Jesus."

"The kitchen door is locked," shouted Dev. He and Zara threw their weight at the door trying to force it open.

On the other side of the room, the doors were splintering.

We're running out of time. A fist-sized knot formed in my stomach.

"The barricade won't hold!" shouted Bruce. He, his brothers, and Grady, backed away from their door.

Karen's shrieking cut off as her voice went hoarse.

"Move!" Sai shoved Reed and I toward his siblings.

Zara and Dev backed away from the kitchen door while Grady tried kicking it in with his steel-toed boots.

Thud. Thud.

Hank and Ed Richardson joined him. They smashed halfway through the wood, but it wasn't enough.

We'll never get through in time.

Reed's legs buckled and he sagged to the floor.

"Reed, get up!"

He stared at me with unfocused eyes.

"Please!" *Oh, God.* We needed a miracle.

The metal service hatch on the wall near the buffet tables caught my eye. The three-foot by three-foot rolling hatch served as a pass through to the kitchen. "Guys! Use that!"

"Good thinking." Sai ran to the hatch. It rolled up with a yank of his hands. He poked his head inside. "It's clear! Zara, Dev, we can get in through here!"

Shoving Zara out of the way, Grady rushed over to the hatch.

Sai glared at him. "It's ladies first."

"Fuck that." Grady body-checked Sai and dove through.

The Richardson brothers scrambled through the hatch after him.

"Zara, Lee!" Sai shouted.

His brother and sister ran over just as the far door splintered inward.

Zombies tried to rush into the cafeteria, but there were too many of them crushing together. For a brief moment, they trapped themselves in the doorway.

Evan, Janelle, and the firefighters ran over.

"Go! Go! Go!" Sai shouted, shoving his sister and then his brother through the hatch.

Janelle pushed past me and climbed through with Evan right on her heels.

Eric and Ben stopped to get Karen.

She was like a statue, her muscles locked in place.

Eric threw the heavy woman over his shoulder and ran her to the hatch. "Climb through," he shouted to her.

She refused to move.

"Push her through to me," Ben ordered, sliding through the hatch.

"Come on, Karen." Eric tried to yank the empty wine bottle out of her hands.

Zombies poured into the room.

"Eric, get in here now!" Ben cried.

Eric abandoned Karen and jumped through the opening.

A moment later the two firefighters disappeared somewhere inside the kitchen.

Sai grabbed me. "Your turn."

"I'm not going without Reed." A burst of adrenaline gave me the strength to yank my lover to his feet.

Reed stood on shaking legs and swayed into me. It looked as if he was having a hard time keeping his eyes open.

There was no way he could climb through the hatch by himself. We'd have to go with the firefighters' idea. "Sai, go in and I'll shove him at you."

Sai looked as if he wanted to argue, but more Biters staggered into the cafeteria, tripping over the tables in their path.

"Hurry!" I pleaded.

Sai jumped through the hatch at the same time shouting came from deep inside the kitchen.

"They're zombies in here!" Zara screamed over the sound of pots and pans hitting the floor. I could see her and Dev grabbing Sai's arm. "Fall back! Fall back!"

"Lee!" Sai gave me a frantic look and tried to grab my hand, but his siblings dragged him away.

A moment later, Biters filled the space where he'd stood.

I pulled Reed away from the hatch as clawing hands shot out of the opening from the kitchen side.

The sound of gnashing teeth drew my attention to the dozens of zombies staggering toward us. The tables were slowing them down, but eventually they'd get to us.

My gaze bounced around the room as I searched desperately for a way out.

There was nothing. No miracle. Just more and more zombies staggering in. Filling the air with the scent of their putrefying flesh.

Gagging on the smell, I shoved Reed into the corner of the room by the Christmas tree. He fell to the floor, his body wracked with tremors. "I-I'm so sorry, Lee."

Karen, who I'd almost forgotten about, let out a hoarse scream.

I grabbed her arm and tried to shove her into the corner with Reed. As she stumbled back, the bottle of wine fell out of her hands and smashed onto the linoleum floor.

The shattered neck of the bottle was still in one piece. Without even thinking, I grabbed the makeshift weapon and held the jagged end toward the slow-moving army of dead.

It was ludicrous to think fighting a few of them off would make any difference, but I had to try.

"We're going to die!" Karen cried, shaking free of her temporary paralysis.

I snatched another jagged piece of glass off the floor and pressed it into her hand. "Protect him!" I pushed her at Reed.

Reed mumbled something, but I couldn't hear him over the clicking teeth. The dead were only a few feet away.

I kicked off my platform heels and sank into a defensive crouch. *Wouldn't Dominic be proud of me?* I thought hysterically.

I felt a fleeing sense of regret that I'd never see Sergeant Pain in the Ass or Avi again.

Behind me, Karen made a choking sound.

Reed shouted my name.

But I couldn't turn around because the dead were closing in.

My heart pounded so fast it nearly beat out of my chest.

The dead lurched forward, their fish belly-white faces blurring together.

A scream lodged deep in my throat, but I locked my lips, refusing to let it out. I would not die screaming.

I'll fight until my very last breath.

A massive six-and-a-half-foot tall zombie staggered ahead of the others. His head was canted to the side, but I recognized his pale face and blood-covered army fatigues.

Dominic.

Oh, God.

Fresh blood dripped from the dead sergeant's mouth as if he'd already fed on someone. A low rattling moan escaped his lips.

No.

Not him.

A soul-shattering grief tore at me, and tears burned my eyes. Knowing I had to give him the mercy of a final death before I was torn apart, I raised my broken bottle. Then I let out a battle cry and rushed straight at him.

No part of me expected him to catch my wrist in the air.

Terrified, shocked, and confused, I met his unclouded, midnight gaze.

He's not a zombie...

Keeping one hand shackled around my wrist, Dominic made a motion with his other hand.

The zombies in the room straightened, some of them throwing off the gore-caked blankets I only now realized they'd been wearing over their clothes.

The bottle neck fell out of my hand as I struggled to make sense of what was happening.

Familiar faces broke out in grins around the room.

Nikki waved at me from over by the door while Paula, Jerry, and Roger scrubbed the dirt and makeup off their faces.

"Damn, hooker's got some balls. Did you see how she went for Sarge?" a tall female zombie, I now recognized as Darcy said to the male soldier next to her.

Mike, who I could only place from his blond crew-cut, grinned. "I bet on yellow team. Does this mean they win?"

Win?

"Hell, yeah it does," Enrique exclaimed from the far side of the cafeteria. On closer inspection, the blood covering him was too bright to be real.

"No, it does not," Dominic said flatly. "Both teams fail the test."

Test?

A sinking feeling slithered through me. "Was this one of your tests?"

Dominic nodded and dropped my wrist. "To pass it, you and the others needed to get out to the courtyard in less than five minutes."

"Don't feel bad," Roger called out. "None of the people in the classrooms made it out either."

"I-I thought we were going to die," I whispered, emotion burning my eyes.

"You would have died fighting." Dominic nodded his head in a rare show of approval. "A good soldier dies on their feet."

My adrenaline crashed, leaving me weak and shaking.

"Um, Sarge, we have a problem," Darcy said, peering around us. "Isaac, get your ass over here."

I twisted around to follow her line of vision.

Reed cradled Karen's body in his arms next to the tree. His shaking hands were pressed against the heavy-set woman's neck. Blood poured from between his fingers.

"Karen cut herself," Reed choked out. "She said she didn't want to be eaten."

Isaac, a former EMT, rushed from the doorway over to them. He had Reed move his hands so he could inspect the wound.

Blood sprayed all over Isaac, Reed, and the Christmas tree.

Isaac shook his bald head. "She cut her carotid. There's nothing we can do."

A cry went up somewhere in the room. I heard Tori call out, "Mom! Is my mom okay?"

Dominic cursed. "We took their weapons to prevent something like this from happening."

Guilt suffocated me. I'd given Karen the shard of glass. I was responsible for this.

"You can let go now," Isaac said softly to Reed.

Reed gently set Karen's lifeless body down at the base of the Christmas tree.

Blood dripped from an ornament onto Karen's face.

My senses cut through Tori's wailing and the low murmurs of the people in the room, zoning in on that one sound.

Plip.

Plip.

In my mind, Karen's sightless blue eyes turned brown. Her features morphed into my mother's face.

Daddy, no!"

"Stop!"

"Mommy!"

Avi called my name from far away, but the flashback had me tightly in its grasp and it carried me kicking and screaming into the darkness.

"Congratulations Sarge, you broke her," I growled. "Happy now?" Under normal circumstances, I'd never show such disrespect to a commanding officer, much less a Titan soldier like my mother. But these weren't normal circumstances, and it was Lee he'd destroyed.

Impulsive, reckless, arrogant, stubborn, all too human Lee. Her breathtaking beauty made her a threat to my brother's heart, and her fierce spirit made her a threat to mine.

Sarge swung his gaze from the catatonic female on his couch to me. The look in his eyes was so bleak, it almost made me reevaluate everything I knew about the legendary warrior.

He was reputed to be ruthless and emotionless, but right now he looked like a man being torn apart. That made no sense because he'd done nothing but treat Lee with disdain and ridicule since day one.

She was a human female with emotional baggage and a chip on her shoulder a mile wide. She wasn't one of his battle-hardened soldiers. *What did he think would happen?*

"Shut your mouth, Lykos," Mike sneered, coming to the sergeant's defense. My presence unsettled him. Very few of my kind were still in active duty, and with very rare exception, all were paired with Titan handlers. I had my mother to thank for my freedom along with the irritating band of silver I wore around my left bicep. The silver weakened me, made me impotent, and kept me from shifting into a wolf. However, it also provided a loophole that kept me out of military conscription.

Well, it had until recently. Sarge seemed to have enlisted me anyway. At least I could still watch over my siblings here at the school, not that they were really appreciating my presence in their lives right now. I'd unleashed hell on them for leaving Lee behind in the cafeteria. Tactical exercise or not. I'd taught them better than to abandon someone in need of protection.

Maybe if they'd stayed with her she wouldn't have ended up like this. A hollow feeling opened up in my chest as I raked my gaze over Lee.

She lay as if frozen on the leather couch in Sarge's office where she'd been for the past three hours. In that time, she hadn't moved a muscle. Not even a flicker of her eyelashes.

Her eyes were the hardest to look into. I longed to see sparks of life in those deep brown orbs, instead I saw complete and utter emptiness.

I wanted to be unmoved by her state, but it was impossible. During the ten days we'd been at the school, the female had wormed her way into my family. First Zara, then Sai, then even naïve Dev had fallen into her orbit. I'd fought my attraction to her. *Hell.* I'd fought it tooth and claw.

It was best for me and my family not to form attachments to outsiders. We needed to stand together to survive the world right now. Even though my siblings were human, instead of Lykos like me, they had a Titan for a mother which meant they were part of a world most humans couldn't comprehend.

But in less than two weeks, Lee had shattered that dividing wall between us. She'd made my family care for her. She'd made me care for her.

But what did that bring me? Nothing but the pain of watching her retreat into herself. My hands curled into fists as I forced my gaze from her to my sergeant.

The Titan paced back and forth, scraping his hands through his short hair. If I didn't know better, I'd think Sarge was in love with Lee. But that was impossible seeing as how he was mated to one of my mother's closest friends. Titans, much like Lykos, mated for life.

"She should have snapped out of this by now," Sarge exclaimed.

Is he a total idiot? "Obviously, she had some kind of psychotic break."

Sarge flinched, something close to guilt flashing in his eyes.

"It's temporary," Mike said, way too flippantly. "She's probably just upset about that civilian killing herself."

Although seeing Karen bleed out had traumatized more than a few civilians, Lee seemed made of stronger stuff. There was something else going on.

"I think the experience triggered her PTSD," Sarge announced, surprising both me and Mike.

"PTSD?" the other Titan echoed.

Sarge nodded. "She has all the signs. Flashbacks. Hyper-vigilence. Overactive fight or flight."

Mike gave him a pensive look. "Eden mentioned her mother, father, and sister died when she was a child."

"Gather more intel," Sarge ordered, straightening his

shoulders. "The past could be the key to unlocking this." He waved his hands in Lee's direction all the while keeping his face averted as if he couldn't handle seeing her this way.

I could hardly bear it either. But I forced myself to look at her so I could report back to Lee's family.

"Eden and Reed have been asking to see her." Begging, pleading, and demanding was more like it, not that Sarge would care.

"They can see her tomorrow," Sarge snapped.

I clenched my fists tighter reigning in the urge to shout at how asinine it was to keep Lee from the people who loved her most. They were probably the only ones who could bring her out of this.

I let out a deep breath. "Speaking of tomorrow, the Richardsons were hoping you would say some words at Karen's funeral."

Sarge frowned. "Funeral? I didn't authorize a funeral."

Mike smacked him on the shoulder, a move that showed how close the two Titans were. "Honoring the dead is important for humans. It'll help bring some morale back." He didn't add that the mood at the school was at an all-time low. Sarge's tactical training exercise had backfired big time.

"Several members of red team are talking about deserting," I felt compelled to add.

Sarge's eyes narrowed. "The hell they are."

"The Richardson brothers aren't happy." More specifically, their wives were furious over Karen's death and they blamed Sarge.

Mike cursed.

Sarge ground his teeth together. "I'll go talk to them." He looked over at Mike. "Find your mate and get insight into her and Lee's trauma. We need to know what happened to them as children."

Eden is Mike's mate? Only years of self-control kept me from showing my surprise. It was unheard of for a Titan to be mated to a human. Titans were mated to Titans and Lykos were mated to Lykos which was why I would always remain single.

Mike nodded.

I turned to follow both men out, but Sarge held up his hand. "Avi, stay here and watch over her." He motioned at Lee.

"But I'm still on patrol." And staying here with the corpse-like version of the female who starred in every one of my fantasies was the last thing I wanted to do.

"Stay," my sergeant snarled.

"Yes, sir." As I'd advised Lee yesterday, sometimes it was better to bend than break.

After the Titans left, I let out a deep breath. Being around their kind always put me on edge. I felt as if I had to constantly be on guard in case they tried to pair me with a handler. I couldn't imagine anything more horrible than having my free will stripped from me and becoming a Titan's attack dog.

Lucky for me, Sarge was the only trained handler here and based on the biometric scanner on his arm, he was already paired with a beast—a beast I sensed was in this very office.

Keeping one eye on the door, I walked behind the desk and inspected the male lying under the blanket.

It had to be some kind of shifter. However, its strange features, lack of scent, and enormous size made it impossible to identify. Even more disturbing, it appeared to be in a coma and completely unresponsive to my presence.

Did Sarge inflict this state on the shifter as punishment or had it been traumatized like Lee?

Not sure I wanted to know the answer, I re-covered the male with the blanket and strode back to Lee's side.

She was so beautiful, looking at her made my insides ache. Which was strange because I normally wasn't attracted to good-looking women. In my experience, the prettier the outside, the more rotten the core. But that wasn't the case with Lee.

For all her faults, she was willing to sacrifice herself for the people she loved and that set her apart from most of the humans I'd encountered in my life.

But it wasn't just her looks or her selflessness, it was her very essence down to her sweet, lush scent that called to me. No other female had ever captured my attention like Lee. During those rare stolen moments when I removed my silver band to jerk off, it was always her I imagined being with.

I never dreamed she'd feel the same attraction, but while I'd been digging her ditch, she'd given me a look of desire and damn if that didn't drive me crazy.

But there was nothing I could do about it. Even if she weren't in some waking coma, I couldn't be with her. Years ago, I'd sworn never to take a lover. I couldn't risk anyone discovering what I was.

The silver made me impotent anyway. I tugged at the band around my bicep in frustration. It was a constant drain on my energy and wearing it put me in a perpetually foul mood. However, being caught without it on was risky.

Fuck it.

Feeling reckless, I slipped the silver band off and stuffed it into my back pocket. Almost immediately, my energy and strength began to return. Shifting would be ten times more invigorating, but there was no way in hell I'd chance that. Given my luck, Sarge would find me and I'd end up in worse shape than his current beast.

Poor bastard. And poor Lee. She didn't deserve this. Not after how incredibly brave she'd been.

Sitting down next to her, I stroked her silky hair the way I used to do with Zara and Dev when they were young. "Sarge will never admit it, and normally I would never admit it, but you were spectacular back in the cafeteria." The memory of her barefoot and wild-eyed attack of Sarge would be forever seared into my mind.

"I'd promote you to red team based on that alone if I was in charge." Wondering if she could hear me, I added, "Don't blame yourself for what happened to Karen, oak tree. We are all responsible for our own choices in life and death. She chose her way out and she's at peace now." *Unlike the rest of us.*

It could have been my imagination, but I thought Lee's breathing changed.

Almost afraid to get my hopes up, I continued talking. "Eden and Reed are worried about you. I think Reed is blaming himself, he's even sober for the first time since he got here."

Lee's eyelashes fluttered.

"And Sai feels bad for leaving you behind." *As he should.* "You've made a strong impression on him." Wasn't that the understatement of the year? "And me." The last two words just kind of slipped out.

Lee coughed and slowly sat up.

I smiled at her. "Welcome back to the land of the living."

The arch look she gave me made me chuckle.

She tried to clear her throat. "W-what happened?" Her voice sounded raspy.

I looked around for some water, but all I could find was a can of unopened orange soda on the side table.

Popping the top, I handed it to her. "You tell me. You've been a statue for the past three hours."

"Three hours?" she echoed. Looking confused and vulnerable, she took a sip of the drink. She closed her eyes savoring the soda. "That tastes so good."

Fuck. Her throaty moan sent all the blood in my body due

south. Since I wasn't wearing the silver band, my cock stood at attention.

"Is everyone okay? I mean, everyone other than Karen?"

"Everyone is fine," I said, slouching forward to hide my erection.

"That's a relief." Lee looked around. "Why are we in Dominic's office?"

"Because he brought you here." I didn't add that he'd refused to let anyone else touch her or see her, not even the nurse.

"And where is Sergeant Pain in the Ass?"

I motioned at the door. "Trying to give some comfort to Karen's family."

Lee scoffed. "Like he's capable of giving anyone comfort."

I hid my smile although she wasn't wrong. "Karen's death seemed to upset you, oak tree. Why? You two weren't close."

Lee sighed and pushed back her tangled curtain of hair. "Seeing her die under the Christmas tree triggered some bad memories."

"Mmm-hmm." I waited for her to say more.

She picked at the cuticle on her thumb.

A heavy silence fell between us. I didn't try to fill it.

Just when I was sure she wouldn't say anything, she blurted out, "When I was a kid, my father, who was a Special Forces soldier, went on a rampage and killed my mother and older sister. It happened a few days before Christmas. Sometimes when I see things that remind me of that night, like a blood-covered Christmas tree, it triggers a flashback."

"You need to get a handle on that. There's a lot of blood-covered Christmas shit outside the school." I motioned toward the front gates.

Her injured look told me I'd screwed up. I swallowed hard and tried to think of how my smooth-talking younger brother would respond. Sai would focus on her feelings. I cleared my throat. "That must have been a hard thing to live through."

She gave me a watery smile, her eyes brimming with tears. *Oh, fuck no. Is she going to cry?*

Lee took a deep breath and closed her eyes. When she opened them again, her tears were gone. "Yes, that's why I'm so protective of the family I have left."

"That makes sense." Finally, I understood what made her tick. And damn if it didn't make me fall harder for her.

"Speaking of family, I need to see Reed and my sister." She set the can down on the table and jumped to her feet. She must have moved too fast because her knees immediately buckled. She tried to catch herself on the edge of the table but ended up sprawled over me.

"Oh, crap." She tried to push herself out of my lap and got a handful of my cock.

Wincing, I helped her sit upright.

Her face flushed. "I'm sorry. Did I hurt... um... you?"

"Yeah, want to kiss it and make it feel better?" As soon as my smart-ass comment left my lips, I wanted to kick myself in the balls. I stood. "Forget I said that. I'm going to..." *stick my head in the shit bucket, have Sai beat me with his war hammer, go anywhere that isn't here...* "... get back to my patrol," I finally said.

Sarge's order to watch over her wasn't relevant since she was awake. She was his problem to deal with now. I turned to leave, but Lee grabbed one of my belt loops and held me in place.

"What if I wanted to kiss it?" she said in a husky voice. The sultry look she gave me through her lashes blanked my mind.

She can't mean what I think she means.

She yanked me closer, her fingers going to my waistband.

I went as still as she'd been ten minutes ago.

She worked the button on my fly open.

Oh, fuck.

I shouldn't. I'd sworn an oath. But here... now... with her, I was suddenly willing to break it.

I groaned as she dragged my fly down.

Very willing.

17

LEE

I don't know what possessed me to proposition Avi. Maybe it was because I'd had a near death experience and I now wanted to live life to the fullest. Or maybe it was because sharing the worst experience of my life made me feel closer to him. I'd never felt comfortable sharing that story with anyone, but there was something about Avi that put me at ease.

It was as if he saw me as I was—the good and the bad. Reed only seemed to see my good qualities. Sometimes I felt as if he'd built me up to be this perfect woman in his mind. Something I could never hope to live up to. In contrast, Dominic only saw my bad qualities. I'd never be good enough for Sergeant Pain in the Ass, not that I wanted any part of him.

Avi saw my flaws and, although he was still a judgmental bastard, he didn't fault me for them. Also, he'd been so gentle in the way he'd stroked my hair. No one had shown me tenderness like that before. Mostly because I wouldn't let them, but that was beside the point.

Avi wanted me, and badly if that tree branch in his pants

was any indication. And I wanted to reward him for being there for me the way no one else had been.

Avi's breathing hitched as I slowly opened his jeans. His erection sprang free and bobbed in front of my face. He was long, hard, and ready.

"Commando. Why am I not surprised?" I wondered what his reaction would be if he knew I was going commando too.

Avi made an inarticulate sound. His concentration seemed focused on my fingers trailing across his skin. The hard muscles of his lower abs jumped under my fingertips.

Smiling up at him, I wrapped my hand around his shaft. It felt like a hot brand against my fingers. I tugged off my gloves so I could feel him skin to skin.

"I'm so glad you're normal-sized." I cast my gaze over toward Hunter and his monster-cock.

Avi stilled. "Are you saying I don't measure up?" He pulled away.

Ah, hell. I'd gone and insulted the guy. *Way to go, Lee. Isn't like the first rule of sex to make the guy feel like he has a big dick?* I grabbed the side of his jeans before he could zip them up.

"It's perfect. I've only been with one guy a couple of times. I don't have a lot of experience."

"Really?" Avi said, looking as if he didn't believe me.

"I've never even given a blow job before. Would you be my first?"

Avi's throbbing cock answered for him. Fluid beaded on the smooth purple tip.

Reacting on pure instinct, I leaned over and licked it off. The salty-sweet taste was different. Not bad. Not good. Just different.

Avi took a swift intake of breath. He swelled even more.

I giggled. "I'll take that as a yes."

"Yes, fuck yes." He threaded his hands through my hair and pushed himself against my lips.

I sucked him inside my mouth.

His entire body seized as if hit with fifty volts. His hands fisted my hair as if he wanted to drag me away, but his hips jerked forward.

I tentatively slid my tongue around the engorged head. When I hit a spot just underneath the tip, tremors went through him. I laved him there.

He let out a sexy groan.

It turned me on seeing him like this—every sinew and tendon taut with lust. Wetness pooled between my legs and I sucked him harder.

His hips thrust back and forth in time with my mouth, he seemed to want me to go faster.

In trying to increase the pace, I accidentally scraped him against my teeth.

He grunted.

I pulled away. *Crap. Am I even doing it right?* All I had to go on were conversations I'd had with Cami. According to her, swallowing was a big deal.

As if sensing my anxiety, Avi glanced down. "You're doing amazing."

Well, okay then. Gaining confidence, I sucked his shaft back into my mouth and worked him with my tongue and lips.

He threw his head back. "With your hand."

Careful to avoid my blisters, I moved my fist up and down in concert with my mouth.

"Oh, fuck." His groans became more guttural. Then he jerked away. "I'm going to cum."

I positioned my lips over him. "Go ahead."

His breath sawed in and out and his body trembled, but he fed his cock back into my mouth.

I relaxed my throat so I could take him deeper, the way Cami had always advised.

He moaned, his thrusts getting wilder and faster.

Fighting against my gag reflex, I gave myself over to the moment—I gave myself over to him.

He shouted my name. Then his hips jerked, and he coated the back of my throat with his salty-sweet flavor. I drank it all down, loving how he shuddered over me.

In the past, I'd always viewed the act as degrading, but I didn't feel degraded. I felt feminine, powerful, and full of desire.

Before I could ask if he'd drop to his knees and return the favor, the office door slammed open.

Dominic stalked into the room, his eyes brimming with black fire. "Mother of Christ. What are you doing?"

"Isn't it obvious?" I said around Avi's softening cock.

Avi cursed. "Uh... Sarge. You're back sooner than expected." He jerked away and zipped up his pants.

Dominic's nostrils flared as Avi spun around. "I told you to watch over her, not shove your dick in her mouth."

"But I wanted his dick in my mouth." I grabbed Avi's arm and used it to pull myself to my feet. I was barefoot, but given how my legs trembled, it was probably a good thing I didn't have those platform heels on.

"You're not helping," Avi whispered.

Dominic's mouth opened and closed as if he was struggling for air. His eyes landed on the open bottle of orange soda. "That's mine."

"And now it's mine," I said calmly wiping my lips.

Avi gave me an incredulous look. "Don't poke the bear, oak tree."

But that bear had pushed me to the brink. He'd made me think Reed and I were going to die. He'd killed Karen. Or rather, he'd put her in a situation where she'd felt she had no choice but to kill herself, which was the same thing.

Dominic's jaw ticked. "As part of our bargain you agreed to park the attitude, Ms. Walker."

Avi looked between us. "Bargain?"

Completely exhausted, I took the high road. "Fine. I apologize for drinking your soda, sir. I will bring you a replacement at my earliest convenience, sir."

Dominic didn't look the slightest bit placated. "You will not engage in sexual relations with Avi or anyone else while at the school."

Avi tensed. "Sarge—"

"Return to your patrol, soldier."

A strange rumbling growl escaped Avi's lips.

Dominic and I both jerked in surprise.

What the hell is that?

"I'm not leaving her," Avi said through clenched teeth. "She's been traumatized enough by you today."

The shocked look on Dominic's face would have been humorous if I wasn't so pissed at him.

I rolled onto my toes and kissed Avi's cheek. "Don't worry. I can take care of myself. I'll find you later and we'll continue where we left off."

Avi gave me an uncertain look, so I smacked him on his ass. "Go on, willow tree."

My new lover's eyes nearly crossed. "You did not just do that."

I grinned. "I'll see you and your perfect cock in a few."

Avi shook his head, gave Dominic a warning look, and strode out of the office.

Dominic blinked as if he wasn't sure what happened. "How did you do that?"

"What?"

"Turn him against me. Avi recognized me as his alpha and now..." he trailed off looking at me as if I'd sprouted another head.

I shrugged. "I guess he likes blow jobs better than being yelled at. Go figure."

Dominic gave me an aggravated look. "It can't be a coincidence." He glanced toward Hunter's body. "You've got the last Typhos in existence thinking you're his mate and now you've ensnared a Lykos."

"Typhos? Lykos? What the hell are you talking about?"

Ignoring my confusion, Dominic searched my face. "What are you?"

I sighed. "Really freaking tired, actually. So, if you have no more tests for me tonight. I'd like permission to get some sleep, sir."

The formality in my request had him stiffening. "You may return to your assigned classroom."

"Thanks," I said, trying to bite back the sarcasm. I started for the door, but he stepped into my path.

My hands went to my hips. "Are we really doing this again?"

"Before you leave, I want to know why you have PTSD?"

"I don't have PTSD." I could see the door over his massive shoulder. Escape was so close but so far away.

"I've been in the military a long time. I know it when I see it."

"Fine, I have it and I'm dealing with it." Talking to Avi about that horrible night made me feel a lot better. *Maybe one day I'll tell Avi everything.* My stomach churned at that thought.

Dominic's beautiful lips flattened into a line. "If tonight's zombie attack had been real and you fell into a comatose state like you did, you would have died."

"I would have died anyway," I said, throwing up my hands. "You all surrounded me, remember?"

My words fell on deaf ears. Dominic nodded his head as if he'd come to some brilliant solution. "You'll meet with Roger weekly to resolve this... weakness."

"Weakness?" Only Dominic would traumatize the hell out of a person and then criticize them for falling apart.

"When a true warrior eliminates his weaknesses, not even death can hold him," he recited.

I rolled my eyes. Dominic loved quoting weird shit like that. He acted as if his little sayings were empowering instead of confusing as hell. "And I suppose you're a true warrior, with no weaknesses to be found, right?"

"None," he answered in a flat voice. I had the distinct impression he was lying.

What's his weakness? If I knew what it was, I'd exploit the ever-loving hell out of it.

He frowned, his gaze settling on my mouth. "I don't want you seeing Avi."

I purposefully misunderstood him. "We live together. I'll see Avi every day unless you blind me. Are you planning on blinding me as one of your tests?"

"Don't be ridiculous. You know what I mean."

I tossed back my head so I could glare up at him. "My love life is none of your business. I like Avi. He likes me. And as soon as I leave here, I'm going to find him and screw his brains out."

A choked sound had me glancing around Dominic's massive bicep.

Reed stood in the open doorway, an anguished expression on his face.

Ah, hell.

Dominic glanced back at Reed. "What do you want, Hippie?"

Reed sucked in a harsh breath. "To check on Lee and inform you I'm no longer possessed by Hunter."

Dominic turned to face him. "Is that so?"

Reed nodded. "The drugs are out of my system and I'd hear his voice if he were here. He's gone, sir."

I clapped my hands together. "That's wonderful news."

"Yes," Reed said stiffly, not looking at me.

Shit. He'd totally heard me talking about screwing Avi. *Dammit to hell*.

Dominic glanced in Hunter's direction. "It doesn't appear he's returned to his body."

"Hunter must be possessing someone else then," Reed said, sounding tired.

An icy chill whipped down my spine. *Does that mean Hunter will come after me in a different body?*

Dominic must have detected my change in mood, because he gave me a reassuring look. "Hunter will not harm you as long as you are under my protection. I'm his alpha."

"Didn't you just say that about Avi?" I retorted. It was absolutely the wrong thing to say, because both men scowled at me.

"I'm feeling withdrawals," Reed said, rubbing his hands over his chest. "I'm going back to my room." Without even saying goodbye, he turned and left.

I started after him, but, once again, Dominic blocked me with his brick wall of a body. "It seems we need to amend the terms of our bargain."

"It seems I don't need to bargain with you at all," I threw back. "In fact, maybe we should just leave." A life without Dominic's insane rules and barbaric tests sounded like heaven. I wondered if Avi and his siblings would leave with us.

Dominic frowned. "I'm the only one who can protect you from Hunter. If he believes you're his mate, he won't stop until he claims you."

Claims me? I shuddered, fighting the urge to look at Hunter's body. The idea of running into Hunter again creeped me out. Not knowing what body he'd use to come after me was even freakier. He could possess anyone. Hell, he could bounce from person to person before settling back into his old body and trying to pounce on me with his monster-cock. Or worse, he could go after the people I loved. *Dammit.* I'd be willing to do anything to avoid that. Even make another deal with the devil.

Clearing my throat, I said, "If I stay, you need to butt out of my love life. I'll screw whoever I want to screw."

Dominic's jaw ticked, but he didn't argue.

"And no more unleashing real or fake zombies on me here at the school," I added.

He pursed his lips. "Agreed. However, I expect you to continue following my orders and abiding by the rules."

"Agreed. But no more running laps as punishment."

"Don't push it, Ms. Walker." Dominic stepped out of my way. "You're dismissed."

Infuriating man. "Yes, Sergeant Pain in the Ass," I mumbled under my breath.

"What was that?"

"Yes, sir," I said loudly. Then I walked out the door and went in search of the man who's heart I'd just broken.

18

HUNTER

I didn't know who was more fucked in the head right now, me or Reed.

Me. I decided. *Definitely me.*

For the last week, I'd been trapped inside Reed, unable to communicate with him, but still fully aware of everything that was happening to us. Or not happening as it were.

The cocksucker had done nothing but jack himself up with morphine all day and night. As he'd rolled us in and out of consciousness, I'd been stuck in an everlasting hell that I couldn't escape. And even after all that shit, you didn't see me holding back tears.

"Grow a fucking pair already."

Ignoring me, Reed staggered down the hallway towards the music room. I wished he'd take us somewhere else. I was fucking sick of that trash-filled shithole. I was also sick of Reed acting like a pussy. Case in point, his reaction to overhearing Lee and Dom.

"Stop acting like such a dickless wonder. Our mate is not fucking the Lykos." The perpetually annoyed wolf shifter was the last male we needed to worry about. Sai, his pretty boy brother,

on the other hand, might turn into a genuine threat at some point.

Neither Reed nor I could compete with Sai's looks, fame, or smooth-talking ways. But leave me in a room with him for an hour, and the pretty boy wouldn't be so pretty anymore.

I cackled to myself trying to fight off the barrage of Reed's emotions. But no matter how I tried to ignore them, his anger, grief, and jealousy—came at me like a tsunami.

It really fucking sucked that he could ignore me, but I couldn't seem to ignore him.

"Cocksucker, you're overreacting as usual. She just said that shit to screw with Dom's head." It was fucking brilliant actually. I couldn't think of anything that would drive Dom crazier than the idea of Lee seeking out another shifter. He, and those other entitled Titans, thought they were so much better than us. One day, we'd put them all in their place.

Although Reed didn't respond, he slowed our pace.

"Why did you tell Dom and Lee I was gone?" I asked, curious.

He didn't answer.

"I know you can hear me, cocksucker." It wasn't as if there was an invisible barrier between our minds like before when he was high. In fact, if I summoned enough strength, I could probably take over our body. The thought thrilled the hell out of me.

Reed reached the door to the music room, flung it opened and stepped inside the dimly lit space. Then he finally answered me. *"Because this has to stop. You saw what happened in the cafeteria. We were useless to Lee."*

Fuck. We'd been worse than useless. When the attack first went down, I'd been somewhat excited. I half-hoped that Reed would get taken out. At least that would have ended this never-ending one-way movie. Either I'd be free to find a new body, or I'd evaporate into the ether. Both options seemed better than being trapped in this lifeless limbo.

But then I'd realized the danger to Lee and the lengths she'd go through to save us. As her mate, it was my purpose in life to protect her and keep her safe. Instead, she'd had to give up her chance at survival to protect us.

"She would have sacrificed her life for us," Reed said, his inner voice filled with anguish. *"If that hadn't been a training exercise, she'd be dead like Karen."*

Reed still hadn't gotten over the fat bitch dying on us. He was young and inexperienced with death. Unlike me.

He continued, *"As long as we keep taking morphine, we're a liability to her—to everyone."*

"I could have told you that a motherfucking week ago, cocksucker." In fact, I was pretty sure I had said that.

"I'm done with drugs," he announced.

"Good call." I tried to keep the excitement out of my voice. With no drugs in our system, I'd be able to take control of our body and explain myself to Lee.

I was a strong enough male to admit that I'd fucked up. I should have been clear from the beginning about who I was and who we were to each other. No wonder Lee was furious with me. I'd been so focused on mating her I hadn't managed introductions. And then Dom and Reed had poisoned her against me.

I wasn't the monster they'd made me out to be and if she'd give me another chance, I'd lay the truth down and set this right. I'd tell her everything about who I was, about the army, about the fucked-up shit they'd made me do, and how finding her had been the single best thing to happen to me.

I'd also tell her I was okay sharing her with Reed.

A week had given me enough time to come around to that idea. I mean, it wasn't as if Lee was destined to be mine and mine alone anyway. I was always going to share her with my brother. *What's one more male?* Especially, when that male and I shared a body and, sometimes it felt, one soul.

Are Reed and I fusing together in some fucked up way?

I wished there was someone I could ask, like Ghost, or even Dom.

"Dominic will kill us if he suspects you are still possessing me," Reed said, slapping me with a dose of much needed reality.

He's right. Dom didn't want to help. He just wanted to control me and if he couldn't do that, he'd vanquish me just like he'd done to my brothers.

"We won't let him find out," I said, quickly.

"Lee can't know either," Reed added, squashing my hopes and dreams into pulp.

"But—"

"No, Hunter. She hates you. Like wants you to die kind of hates you. In her mind you raped her."

"I didn't rape her." The idea of hurting any part of my dirty dancer was abhorrent to me. *"What we did was consensual and when she cools down a little, she'll see that. She'll recognize me as her mate, and she'll forgive me."* She had to forgive me.

Reed laughed. *"It's like you don't know her at all. Lee doesn't forgive and she doesn't forget. She wants to keep you suppressed so much she let us become this."* He motioned at the track marks running down the inside of our arm.

"Fuck." He had a point. *"What are you proposing?"*

"I don't suppose you could leave?" he asked hopefully.

"I promise you, if I could, I would." Every attempt to extricate myself from his body failed. I was stuck with him and he was stuck with me.

"Then you'll have to stay in the backseat at all times."

"What?"

"You heard me. No attempting to take control of our body ever again."

At least he acknowledged his body belonged to both of us now. *"And if I don't agree?"*

He glanced over at the piano bench where he was keeping the drugs. "I'll overdose and end this for good."

"That'll destroy Lee."

"She'll get over it," he said, hollowly.

"No. She won't. It's like you don't know her at all," I threw back at him. Lee loved him and Eden more than anything in the world. And, as she'd just demonstrated in the cafeteria, she'd die for him. If Reed committed suicide. She might follow him into death. And that was something I couldn't let happen.

"Fine," I said, knowing I didn't really have a choice. *"But what if I took our body for a ride occasionally?"*

"No," he snapped.

"What if we were in a life or death situation again, like back in the cafeteria. If I'd been in control, I could have saved Lee." I wasn't lying and he knew it.

"Maybe then, and only then," he finally said.

Well, that's something.

A wave of nausea rolled through us.

"Withdrawals," we groaned in unison.

Getting clean was going to hurt like a bitch. Good thing I was no stranger to pain.

Reed cranked our head around to look at the piano bench.

"No," I said emphatically. *"No more morphine."*

"Maybe we should wean off it." He moved us one step closer to the baby grand.

"We're going cold-turkey, cocksucker."

Just as I sensed his resolve crumbling, there was a soft knock on the music room door.

"Reed," Lee's husky voice called out.

"Open the door," I urged.

Reed rubbed at our beard. *"I don't know if I want to see her right now."*

"Of course, we want to see her. Now open the damn door or I will," I threatened.

"You stay in the backseat, asshole," Reed snarled.

Good, he was angry. That was better than anxious. *"Just talk to her. You'll see it was a misunderstanding."*

"Fine." Reed marched us to the door and threw it open.

Lee stood on the other side looking stunning. Her black crop top showed off her sexy belly button ring while her cheetah pants showcased her perfect hips and ass. I wanted more than anything to pin her to the wall and rip those clothes off with my teeth.

"Tell her, she's beautiful," I urged Reed.

"What do you want?" he said instead.

Lee's expression fell.

"Smooth, cocksucker. Real, smooth. Way to treat the female who was willing to die to protect us."

He didn't respond to my jab, but our body stiffened.

"Ask her how she's doing?" Both Reed and I had been worried about her after she'd gone into shock. It didn't help that Dom refused to let us see her. *Prick.*

"Are you doing okay?" Reed asked.

Lee nodded. "I just spaced-out, you know how I do sometimes."

"Yeah," Reed said softly.

Space-outs? I was going to grill him about those the first chance I got.

I sensed Reed wanted to hug her, but he forced our arms to his side.

"Are you okay?" our mate asked, searching our face. "That was pretty intense back in the cafeteria."

Reed let out a bitter laugh. "Intense doesn't even cover it." I sensed him thinking about the fat bitch again.

Lee stepped from one bare foot to the other. I wondered where her shoes were. "Can I come in?"

Reed moved us aside so she could step into the room.

She had to navigate around the growing pile of food wrappers and trash near the music stands. Reed's lack of hygiene this past week disgusted even me and I was nowhere near the neat freak Dom was.

Lee wandered over to the nest of filthy blankets under the piano where we'd been sleeping. "So, Hunter's really gone?"

"Yeah," Reed said, lying far better than I'd imagined he could. "Why did you tell Dominic that you like Avi?"

Fucking hell. "For the last time, cocksucker, she was blowing smoke up Dom's ass." Once mates found each other, they never strayed. Whether she liked it or not, Lee had found her mate. *Me.*

Lee sucked in a breath, her face flushing. "I-um..." she rubbed her hands over her cheetah pants and winced. She looked down at what appeared to be a blister on her right palm.

That's not good. She should have that bandaged. I urged Reed to tell her that, but he was too busy being a drama queen.

He moved us so we were right in her face. "Lee, talk to me."

She looked up to meet our gaze. "I care about you Reed. And I want to be with you."

He stiffened our spine. "But..."

"But I can't be tied down to just one person," she gave us an apologetic look.

"I see," Reed said too calmly.

Motherfucker. She really wants to bone the Lykos. I felt as if someone sucker punched me.

Lee grabbed our arm. "I want you to be okay with this."

That pushed Reed over the edge. "Okay with what? You screwing other dudes?"

"With us having an open relationship."

"As in we both screw other people?"

"If that's what you want," she said, looking as if she had a bitter taste in her mouth.

Reed shook our head. "That isn't what I want. I only want you. I've only ever wanted you." He cupped her face in our hands and gazed down at her. "Why isn't that enough? Why aren't I enough?"

"Prove to her she doesn't need another male. Kiss her. Claim her. Mate her until she forgets her own name."

"We can barely stand upright," he reminded me.

He's right. Fuck. A week of drug use had made us weak and impotent. No wonder she'd sought out another male.

Lee couldn't meet our eyes. "I... can't help the way I feel."

"You love Avi?" Reed asked in a choked voice.

"Oh, hell no." Her laugh was harsh. "I can't even stand him half the time, but I'm attracted to him and... other guys too. If tonight taught me anything it's that we don't know how much time we have left. I want to enjoy life before I die, and you should too."

Fuck. Hearing that she wanted other males tore me apart. Maybe this was my fault. If I hadn't mated her in Reed's body things wouldn't have gotten so fucked.

Reed turned us away from her. "Go, do what you need to do."

His pain was my pain, and it battered my soul.

"Reed, please," Lee pleaded.

"Don't pretend you care about what we... what I think. Face it, you're only doing this because you don't want to get too attached to me or anyone else."

Lee's expression grew strained. "You've got me all figured out." She turned and strode angrily toward the door.

"Don't let her walk away. Say yes." Fuck. I can't believe I was the voice of reason here. But any hope of a future between me and my dirty dancer hinged upon us staying together.

Reed sighed. "Don't go."

Lee spun around.

"I love you."

She visibly flinched.

"Are you trying to drive her away, cocksucker?"

"Shut up, Hunter." Reed lifted our hands. "And loving you means that I'd do anything for you. I'd carve my heart out of my chest for you. I'd give up my soul for you. And I'll go along with this open relationship if that's what you really want."

"It is." Lee beamed and ran into our arms.

We hugged her tightly, savoring her closeness.

"Just do me a favor and don't tell me about the other dudes, okay?" Reed said, kissing the top of her head.

"Oh." She pulled back and gave us a wicked smile. "I was kind of hoping for threesomes at some point."

Fuck me.

Just then a searing pain clawed through us.

"Jesus," Reed hissed as we stepped away from her and doubled over.

Lee chewed her lower lip. "Is that too tall an order?"

Reed shook our head. "It's not that. It's tough coming off the drugs."

Lee's eyes filled with concern. "I'm so sorry. What can I do to help?"

Reed pointed our finger at the piano bench. "Take the drugs out of here. Please. I don't trust myself..."

"Of course." Lee rushed over to the bench and grabbed the bag of bottles and syringes. "I'll bring it back to the nurse."

"Thanks," Reed said, through our teeth. Sweat dotted our forehead as a fierce craving hit us.

Lee carried the bag to the door. "I'll see if Sharon has anything to make you more comfortable."

"That'd be good," Reed gritted out. "Will you come back tonight?"

Lee nodded. "And every night. I'll stay here to help you through this, if that's okay."

"Thanks. I could use the support." Reed's even tone was at odds with the giddiness zinging through him.

"Why are you so happy?" I groused, as we watched our mate step out into the hallway. My dirty dancer wanted to bang other males. *Fuck. How am I going to deal with that?*

"How's she going to sleep with other guys when she's staying with us every night?" he replied.

"Good point." Some of my despair faded. *"We need to make this shithole nice for her."* And once our body fully recovered, we'd mate her so hard and so often she'd have no need for anyone else in her life.

In full agreement, we started cleaning.

19

LEE

After the day and night I'd had, I should have been dead on my feet, but I felt surprisingly energized as I headed down the empty hall to the nurse's office. Maybe the bounce in my step was due to my relief that we were free of Hunter. *Thank God.* Or maybe it was because of the adrenaline rush of experiencing so many physical and emotional roller coasters. The latest one being that awkward conversation with Reed. The timing was awful, but I'm glad it happened.

Reed's agreement to an open relationship filled me with such relief. Now I could kiss goodbye to any guilt I might have felt about those passionate moments with Avi in Dominic's office.

I wasn't so thrilled with the idea of the open relationship going both ways though. Just imagining Reed being with another woman made me want to claw someone's eyes out, but I couldn't be a hypocrite. He deserved to explore his sexuality the same way I intended on exploring mine.

For some asinine reason, Dominic's face flashed into my mind.

Nope. Not happening. I didn't care what kind of crazy chemistry burned between us. Sergeant Pain in the Ass was a nightmare. I mean the guy actually made me think I was about to die. He'd driven a woman to suicide. *What kind of evil son of a bitch did that?*

The same guy who'll chew my ass out if he catches me wandering the hallways at this hour.

I glanced around wondering what time it was. The skylights above my head were dark, so I was guessing the middle of the night. Since Dominic didn't allow civilians to sleep in the classrooms on this side of the school, I expected all the rooms I passed to be dark. And they were, except for one.

The flickering light under the computer lab door stopped me in my tracks. Wondering who was inside, I peered through the narrow glass pane in the door. The room was empty, but someone had left a lantern lit on a computer desk. Dominic would lose his shit over someone wasting batteries like that.

I'll shut it off on the way back.

I turned and came face-to-face with a zombie who smelled like the inside of a sewer.

A shriek ripped from my lips. I scrambled back, dropping the baggie of medicine.

Oh, God! Where's my knife? I dug around my waistband searching for the blade that was probably still sitting on the table outside of the cafeteria.

The zombie's rolling eyes fixed on me through the matted hair over its face.

"Help!" I shouted. *Dammit.* There was no one back here but the nurse and her patients. "Help!" I screamed again, hoping Sharon would hear me.

I was fumbling for the handle of the computer door when the zombie belted out, "The Queen is coming! She's coming!"

It's Vincent.

Holy crap. I let out a shuddering breath. That'd been one more shock my poor body didn't need. "Vincent, you can't sneak up on people like that."

"The Queen—the mother of the Kindred—is coming!" The crazy guy's slight frame quivered as if he was terrified.

Despite the horrific smell clinging to his dirt-encrusted poncho, I put my hand on his trembling shoulder. "Don't worry. I won't let her get you."

"She'll smite all those who stand against her," Vincent whispered through a mouthful of broken teeth.

"I'm not so easy to smite." Blinking away his sour breath, I bent down and scooped up the baggie I'd dropped. Thankfully, none of the bottles had cracked.

The sound of thundering footsteps had me glancing up to see Eden, Nikki, Mario, and Sharon charging down the hallway. Each of them brandished a weapon.

I quickly called out, "False alarm. I thought Vincent was a zombie."

Eden lowered her ax, Nikki sheathed her Katana, and Mario tucked his machete into his belt.

Sharon jogged ahead of them with her extra-long, double-pointed, aluminum knitting needle outstretched in front of her. When she got to us, she jabbed her unusual melee weapon at my face. "What are you doing down here?"

I started to show her the baggie, but the steely haired nurse had already turned her attention to Vincent. "Vinnie, what did I say about wandering the halls?"

Vincent licked his cracked lips. "I am a disciple of the queen."

Sharon let out an exasperated sound. The radio in the front pocket of her powder-blue smock-shirt crackled.

Avi's voice called out, "Do you need backup in your sector, Sharon?"

Sharon looked at Mario and mouthed, "Help with Vinnie please?" Then she walked back down the hallway while speaking into the radio in a low voice.

Nikki gave me a wave and followed Sharon.

Mario strode over and grabbed Vincent's arm. "Get your loco ass back to the chapel." As the tattooed man steered him away, Vincent called back to me, "The queen is coming for you, Heaven."

All the hair on my body stood on end. *What the hell? How does he know my first name?* No one at the school besides Eden or Reed even knew it.

"Lee!" Eden exclaimed, ending my momentary freak out.

Deciding that Vincent must have overheard Reed or Eden using that name, I shook off the bum's creepy words and caught Eden as she threw her arms around me.

"I was so worried about you," she cried.

Smiling, I rubbed her back with my free hand. "I can't remember the last time you gave me a hug. Maybe I should scream for help more often."

"Very funny," she said, pulling away. "People were saying you cracked out after the tactical exercise."

I felt my gaze narrowing. "Did you know in advance about that?" If she'd known and hadn't given me a head's up, I'd strangle her.

She shook her head. "No, I swear. I've been here with Rosie all night."

I glanced down the hall. "How is she doing?"

"Good. Sharon thinks it might be a stomach bug, but she's going to keep her for observation along with Kiara. The stress of the fake zombie attack put her into false labor."

"Yikes." That explained Mario's presence in the hallway, but not Nikki's. "What's Nikki doing over here. Was she hurt by Dominic's tactical exercise too?"

"No, she just likes staying with her Grandma. Baba is

rooming with Bernard in the art room," Eden said, mentioning a wheelchair-bound patient of Sharon's. The same patient who'd been without his medicine all week.

A stab of guilt had me holding up the baggie.

"Hey, are those Bernard's meds?"

"Yeah, I wanted to give it back." I handed it to her hoping she wouldn't notice only two bottles still had any liquid in them. "Reed's getting clean."

She gave me a searching look. "Really?"

"Yes. Do you think Sharon has anything that can help with his detox? Nothing too strong. Maybe aspirin or something?"

Eden nodded. "Definitely. I'll find something and run it back to him. Sissy, this makes me so happy." She hugged me again, and I realized just how shitty my decision to take the medication had been.

"I'm sorry," I said, against her silky hair. "I should have listened to you."

Eden laughed. "Can I get that in writing?"

I pulled back to gaze at her. She was normally an inch shorter than I was, but since I was barefoot and she was in thick-soled boots, we were eye-to-eye. "From now on, I'll trust your judgement more, okay?"

Her smile squeezed my heart. "Do you mean that?"

"Absolutely. I love you, Edie." Tears burned my eyes, but they were the happy kind. Maybe we could have that close sister relationship after all.

A clearing throat, had us breaking apart.

Avi stood at the other end of the hallway, giving us a hard look. "Civilians are to be in their assigned classrooms."

The bite in his tone gave me a strange thrill. No one would guess I'd been sucking his dick just a half an hour ago.

"I'll deal with him. Go on, give the meds back to Sharon," I said, shooing Eden toward the nurse's office.

As Eden walked away, Avi strode over. "You need to get to bed."

Damn. He was sexy when he was bossy. He was like a slightly nicer version of Dominic. *Maybe I should start calling him Dominic-lite.*

"But I found something in there," I motioned at the computer lab behind me. "Can I show it to you?"

He gave me a wary look but followed me inside.

I shut the door behind us, locked it, and walked over to the glowing lantern. "Someone left that on. It directly violates safe house rule number six."

"You brought me in here for that?"

"No. I brought you in here for this." I shrugged off my shirt. The cool air whispered against my bare breasts, making my nipples tighten.

Avi's breathing hitched. "Lee, I'm on patrol."

I shimmied out of the leggings, shoved the lantern and keyboard out of the way, and sat back on the desk completely naked. "Fuck me, willow tree."

I savored his moment of stunned silence and then Avi was on me, his hungry mouth crashing down on mine.

I bit his bottom lip as our kiss turned desperate.

Dragging his mouth away, he licked and sucked a scorching path down my neck and chest. He rubbed his face against my breasts, letting me feel the rasp of his stubbled jaw, before sucking on each nipple.

Pleasure sizzled straight to my core. Moaning, I slid my hands under his shirt stroking his ripcord abs.

He thrilled me by yanking his shirt over his head and showing me his mind-blowing body.

I wanted to stroke and lick every inch of his thickly muscled torso, but he stepped out of reach.

My gaze was drawn to a band of metal circling his upper arm. "That's pretty."

"It's an annoying piece of shit." He ripped it off and threw it on the floor. Then he shoved my thighs apart and slid his hand between my legs.

I was embarrassingly turned on and with three strokes of my clit, he sent me spiraling into my first orgasm.

While I shuddered with the aftershocks, he shoved his pants down.

"Where do you want me to put this normal-sized cock?" He brushed the tip back and forth on my clit, making me whimper with need.

"Here." I tried to drag him inside me.

He held back. "I don't have protection."

"Aren't you the guy who is always prepared for anything?" I chided, unable to stop myself from goading him.

"Nothing could have prepared me for you." His gaze sparked with something more than desire, but I was too turned on to care.

"Please," I begged, rocking against him. He was poised right at my entrance, just millimeters from where I needed him.

He shuddered, but still didn't move.

Oh, God. This was worse torture than all those laps Dominic made me run. Trying to eliminate any hang-ups, I panted, "If you're worried about STDs, I've only ever been with Reed and he's only ever been with me. Are you clean?"

"You could say that," he said, the tip of his cock edging a little further inside.

"And I can't get pregnant if that's what you're worried about—" I broke off as he slammed inside me.

"Yes!" I cried at the erotic invasion.

He pulled almost all the way out, grabbed my legs, threw them over his shoulder and thrust into me hard enough to drive my back into the computer monitor behind me.

The monitor careened to the floor with a loud crash, but I was so beyond caring.

Inarticulate sounds escaped my lips as he pounded into me over and over.

"Look at me."

Obeying Avi's order, I stared into his eyes. *Ah, hell.* There was too much emotion glinting in those beautiful hazel depths. All I wanted from him was pleasure. All I could promise him was this moment. Tearing my gaze away, I threw my head back and rocked furiously against his thrusts.

Avi punished me by burying his face into the curve of my neck and biting down. The sharp pain of his teeth sent my pleasure spiraling to dizzying heights.

"Yes! Yes!" I shifted my legs off his shoulder and locked my ankles around his waist. It drove him even deeper.

Avi's hips moved faster and faster until he was thrusting into me with punishing intensity.

It was raw, animalistic, and everything I needed. I clawed his back chasing that inferno of pleasure building inside me. The flames burned brighter and brighter.

I'm so close. So very close.

A shadow flickered across the room.

Over the corded muscles of Avi's neck, I spied Dominic watching us from the hallway. His midnight eyes locked on mine through the window in the door.

Just then, my orgasm hit with the force of a hurricane. The sergeant's hungry gaze held me prisoner as each wave of euphoria crashed through me.

Mindlessly, I screamed Dominic's name.

Avi let out a muffled shout against my sweat-dampened neck. His cock jerked inside me, filling me with his warmth, and his head dropped to my shoulder.

As I struggled to catch my breath, I hoped to hell that Avi hadn't noticed my embarrassing slip up.

Unfortunately, Dominic had. Through the window, he gave me a knowing look. Then the evil son of a bitch smirked and walked away.

❧

The adventure continues with Claiming Her Beasts Book Three (keep reading for a preview)

No one said living through the apocalypse would be easy. I just didn't think it would be this hard.

My sexy beasts seem more interested in fighting each other than fulfilling my increasingly dark and twisted fantasies. Our scorching hot leader is trying to break me with his wicked punishments. And the secret my sister is keeping may destroy us all.

Even worse, our enemies are multiplying, and when our supply run goes south, the price for survival may be too high to pay...

ABOUT THE AUTHOR

Dia wanted to be a writer from the time she could hold a pencil. A lover of paranormal romance, reverse harem, science fiction, urban fantasy, and horror, she writes action-packed stories featuring kick-butt heroines and the alpha male heroes who fall for them.

You can find her books on amazon.

If you want to be notified when the next book in the series releases, please sign up for Dia's newsletter.

You can follow Dia on:
https://diacole.com/
or
Join her reader group:

https://www.facebook.com/groups/1082971415136332

BOOKS BY DIA COLE

CLAIMING HER MATES

Claiming The Nanny

Claiming Her Mates: Book One

Claiming Her Mates: Book Two

Claiming Her Mates: Book Three

Claiming Her Mates Series Collection

CLAIMING HER BEASTS

Claiming Her Beasts: Book One

Claiming Her Beasts: Book Two

Claiming Her Beasts: Book Three

Claiming Her Beasts: Book Four

CLAIMING HER CONSORTS

Claiming the Wardens

EXCERPT FROM CLAIMING HER BEASTS: BOOK THREE

LEE

"It's a good day to die," Zara said, pointing her semiautomatic assault rifle up at the cloudless sky.

My friend's words made the fine hairs on the back of my neck prickle. "Don't say that. Don't even think it." Keeping my fingers tightly wrapped around my tactical knife, I wiped away the sweat on my forehead. It was only New Year's Eve, but the stifling heat wave was a familiar prelude to a scorching Saguaro Valley spring—a spring we probably wouldn't live long enough to see.

Zara swiped her frizzy rainbow curls out of her face and flashed me a feral grin. "We all got to go someday. Why not today?" She moved farther out into the debris-covered street, her face shadowed by the Festival of Lights banner doing the splits between two palm trees overhead.

The banner was yet another reminder that the apocalypse had arrived two weeks before Christmas. Three weeks later, we were still battling the undead in a town forever festooned in the cheerful trappings of my least favorite holiday.

"Hush," hissed Zara's younger brother, Dev. He flattened his back against the abandoned Suburban we were using as cover and glared at Zara through his thick-rimmed glasses. "Get back here if you know what's good for you." At eighteen, he was only a few years younger than Zara and me, but when he acted like this, he reminded me of his bossy older brother.

My lips curled as Avi's rugged face flashed into my mind. Since Christmas, he and I had spent every free moment together. At this point, I knew every square inch of Avi's gorgeous, ripped body better than my own. And yet, I still ached for more of my willow tree's touch, something that was creating tension with my other lover, Reed.

Zara blew a raspberry at Dev. "You're fast becoming my least favorite brother."

"Should I care?" Dev ruined his comeback by sneezing.

As he wiped his nose with his sleeve, Zara snorted and bounced up and down on the balls of her sneakers like the overexcited puppies my sister Eden once rescued. Of course, that had been long before the canine flu vaccine brought about the zombie apocalypse. Now the human species needed rescuing far more than any animals.

"Calm down. You're making me nervous," Dev pleaded. "And I already have a headache. It must be from all the damn pollen." He gave a weak wave of his hand toward one of the Jacaranda trees whose purple bell-shaped blossoms were blooming a full two months earlier than they should. Even the foliage was confused over the crazy as hell weather we'd been having.

Zara rubbed her belly. "Well, I'm starving. Why did we have to skip breakfast for this stupid field training test?"

My stomach rumbled at the reminder of our missed meal. I'd given my sister most of my dinner last night, which made missing the single protein bar we were rationed for breakfast hurt more than usual.

"Shut up, Zara. They'll hear you." Dev jerked his acne

covered chin in the direction of the crowd gathering in front of the Euro Gift Shop down the street.

I tensed, glancing at the mob.

Even with their heads and limbs bent at odd angles, the shambling bodies could almost be mistaken for normal people. But a closer look at their milky eyes, uncoordinated gait, and rotting skin gave them away.

Biters. Zombies. Flesh-eaters.

The tattered army fatigues, hospital gowns, and Southern Arizona University sweatshirts fluttering against putrid flesh were evidence that the town's former citizens had been an eclectic mix of retirees, college students, and military families. In life, those groups may have rarely mingled, but in death, they were inseparable.

Zara scoffed. "They're all the way over there."

She can't be serious.

We all knew how dangerous Biters were when they gathered together, and that horde was one of the largest I'd seen since the day the world went to hell a few weeks ago. The memory of the undead mob smashing through my house had me shivering despite the warm temperature.

Zara held her fingers to her lips and mocked her brother by making loud shushing noises.

Neither the desert heat nor Zara's cavalier attitude was doing anything to thaw the ice water running through my veins.

Why did I volunteer for this? Oh wait. I didn't.

Sergeant Dominic Rosario, the ruthless leader of our group, ordered us to accompany him on this training mission. Before he'd left to scout ahead, he'd announced we'd be tested on our survival skills and our knowledge of his rules.

Ugh. He has so many goddamn rules.

Living under Dominic's command kept us alive, but sometimes I wondered if we'd embraced the devil to survive hell.

I rubbed a sweaty palm on my jeans. *I have to pass his test.* Those that failed were exiled or assigned the most menial jobs back at the school where we were staying. Although being shackled with the sanitation team wasn't the end of the world, being thrown out of the safe house without the protection of Dominic and his soldiers might be. Especially since I had a body snatching demon after me.

I shuddered at the thought of the comatose, ten-foot-tall beast lying on the floor of Dominic's office. Hunter was supposed to be under Dominic's control, but he'd somehow slipped the sergeant's leash to possess Reed and take my virginity.

A familiar wave of disgust and anger pulsed through my body. Hunter had violated me, and I wanted to see him burn. Thankfully, he'd been vanquished from Reed's body, but Dominic warned that Hunter would continue to stalk me, perhaps in the guise of a different body.

I shivered, bile rising in my throat.

As if sensing my fear, two of the Biters down the street lifted their heads and sniffed the air.

I froze, not daring to move a muscle.

After a tense moment, the creatures turned back to their shambling.

I let out a relieved breath.

"Those Biters have the right idea. We should get break-fast there." Zara pointed at the gift shop. "They have the most amazing fruitcakes. They're even better than sex." She smacked her lips. "Come on, Dev. Get one with me."

"No way."

"What about you?" Zara turned to me. "We all know you enjoy fruitcake." She winked, referencing Reed's nickname around the school.

Dev gritted his teeth. "No one is getting a fruitcake with you. Stop acting crazy."

Zara flipped him off.

Dev and I shared a troubled look. Although sassy as hell, the pixie-sized woman's survival skills and razor-sharp focus during training drills had earned her a spot on Dominic's coveted red team. Her strange behavior was only making my anxiousness grow.

"I'm getting breakfast." Zara spun on her heel and marched down the street.

⚜

HAS ZARA LOST HER DAMN MIND?

"Stop her," Dev begged. "She listens to you more than me."

I wasn't sure that was true, but I ran after my friend and snagged the strap of her weapon with my free hand. "Do you have a death wish?"

Zara winked at me and mouthed, "Play along." The overpowering scent of rum wafted off her clothes.

I gasped in disbelief. *We're out in one of the deadliest parts of the neighborhood, and she's drunk? Great. Just great.* Not only weren't we going to pass the field training test, but she was going to get us killed. I cast a quick glance at the Biters. Thankfully, they hadn't detected our presence. *Yet.*

"Let me go," she shouted, trying to shake me off.

Years of spinning around a pole, along with Dominic's daily defensive trainings, gave me the strength to reel the smaller woman in. I dragged her behind an overturned gray sedan, trying to ignore the blood-streaked windows. "Dominic ordered us to stay by the Suburban." *Rule of survival number one, follow Dominic's orders.*

Zara gave a dramatic eye roll. "He's been gone too long. He's probably been eaten."

My stomach dropped. *Not Dominic. He can't die.* Despite my

conflicting feelings for the handsome sergeant, I couldn't bear to consider anything bad happening to him. I shook off her words. "Seriously? He can take out a horde with his bare hands. You don't want to piss him off."

Zara scoffed. "Just because you have the hots for one of the scariest mofos still alive on this planet doesn't mean I'm going to roast my lady balls off waiting for him." She whipped around and elbowed me in the gut.

I doubled over with a grunt, losing my grip on her. "Why the hell did you do that?"

She glared at me with her hands on her hips. "I'm getting that fruitcake."

"Not only is that suicidal, you know we're never supposed to travel anywhere alone." *Rule of survival number eight, always travel with backup.*

She arched a brow. "So, come with me."

Movement over her shoulder quickened my pulse. Two zombies peeled off from the pack and lurched our way. "Biters, eight o'clock!"

The closest flesh-eater was female. She wore teal medical scrubs and an ID badge linking it to the retirement home up the street. The shredded skin of her throat revealed a half-eaten trachea, the same color as her sunken white eyes.

Close behind it shambled a hulking, male Biter, wearing a blue polo and bloodstained chinos. Maggots danced in and out of the gaping hole where his nose had once been.

I gulped. These Biters weren't like the toothless, armless ones we'd practiced fighting back at the school. *These monsters will fight us to the death.*

Zara spun around, her eyes narrowing. "I'll teach these cock blockers to get between me and my breakfast." She shouldered her rifle and pointed it at the female Biter.

"What are you doing?" I grabbed the weapon and ripped

it from her hands. "Guns are only used as a last resort." *Rule of survival number five.* "The noise will attract the others."

"You're right. Damn, I forgot my spear. Can you handle them?"

Crap! I gave Zara her rifle back and shoved her behind me.

The Biter was only a few yards away. Seeing us, she clicked her bloodstained teeth together in frenzied anticipation.

Oh, God! My heart hammered so hard I thought it'd burst through my chest like some kind of alien monster. As fear consumed me, I felt myself starting to space-out. Darkness edged my vision as ghostly terrors of my past threatened to suck me in.

"Snap out of it, Lee!" Zara whispered hoarsely. "Do something or we'll die."

She's right. Forcing away the nightmares in my head, I focused on the nightmares in front of me. I took a deep breath and immediately choked on the pungent, rotting-meat stench of the approaching zombie. Quickly switching to mouth breathing, I focused on Dominic's training. The words he'd drilled into my mind came back to me.

Attack. Don't react.

Stiffening my shoulders, I raised my knife and ran at the flesh-eater head-on.

She opened her jaws and reached for me.

Avoiding the creature's long, jagged fingernails, I stabbed my blade straight through its milky eye. It exploded like an overripe grape.

Ugh. I ripped my blade free, and the flesh-eater collapsed to the street, lifeless.

Before I could congratulate myself on the kill, the male Biter shambled over the corpse and tackled me to the asphalt.

Shit! The air whooshed out of my lungs and my knife flew out of my hand.

"Kick him off!" Zara cried.

Adrenaline roared through me as I fought to keep the Biter's snapping jaws away from my neck.

"You've got this, Lee. You've got this!" Zara chanted, suddenly becoming my personal cheerleader.

No, I don't. He's too strong. My arms shook with the strain of trying to hold off the freakishly huge creature.

He gnashed his teeth, and several writhing maggots fell onto my face.

Oh, God! I couldn't stop the impulse to shake them away. I lost my grip on the Biter.

He went for my throat.

Zara swung the butt of her rifle into the side of his face, knocking him off me.

I scrambled away as she brought the rifle down on his forehead, crunching in its skull like an eggshell.

"Th-thanks," I stammered, wondering why she'd waited so long to help.

She let out a heavy sigh. "You may not thank me in a few minutes. Just remember whatever happens, it'll be okay."

I stared at her in confusion. "What will be okay?"

Ignoring my question, she glanced up at Dev, who'd jogged over to join us.

He sneezed and offered me his hand.

"I'm good. Thanks." Despite Dev's insistence he just had allergies, I suspected he'd caught the cold that was making its way through the safe house. Getting sick was the last thing I needed. Dominic's trainings kicked my ass as it was, and the sergeant didn't allow days off for sickness.

"Better luck next time," Dev said, coughing into his elbow.

"Assuming there is a next time," Zara added, shaking her head. "This was your field training test, girl."

I blinked in slow understanding. "Wait, you mean you guys staged this?"

They shared a guilty look.

"I don't understand. Aren't you being tested today, too?"

"We passed our field training already," Zara replied in an apologetic tone.

"Oh." I tried to smother the bitter feeling of betrayal, but I couldn't meet Zara's gaze.

"Please don't be mad. Dominic didn't give us a choi—" Zara broke off as an enormous shadow fell over us.

My breathing went choppy as I spied all six-foot-six muscular inches of Dominic standing a few yards away. His dark close-cropped hair, tactical vest lined with throwing knives, and shiny black combat boots marked him as the Special Forces soldier he was.

As always, the sight of him filled me with the insane urge to fling myself into his massive arms—arms that would sooner choke the life out of me than embrace me.

"You three, over here." His deep voice rumbled like thunder.

Not wanting to test the sergeant's limited patience, we hustled to follow him down the street.

A small gasp of surprise escaped my lips when I saw the carnage in front of the gift shop. The entire pack of Biters lay motionless on the ground—a single knife wound in the center of their skulls. Dominic's calling card.

As I stepped over the piles of bodies, I realized Dominic must've been inside the shop watching us the entire time. No wonder the Biters were gathering around it.

Way to be observant, Lee.

Dominic's black as pitch eyes drilled into mine as he propped the door to the shop open. The ever-present dark scowl on his sinfully full lips should've been enough to dampen my attraction. But despite his dangerous aura, or maybe because of it, he stirred my hormones the way few men ever had.

I met his gaze boldly, just as I did during his trainings, briefings, or when he watched me have sex with Avi. Truth be told, I didn't enjoy screwing Avi half as much if Dominic wasn't observing in the shadows.

What's wrong with me?

Dominic lived to browbeat people, and still I lusted after him. *Why?* It defied all reason. The one thing I knew was that I'd never let him, or anyone else, intimidate me.

As I stood there, refusing to give him the submission I knew he was seeking, Dominic's stare turned to a glare.

"Inside. Now."

A sinking feeling grew in the pit of my stomach. *Crap. I've failed his test.*

DID YOU ENJOY THIS PREVIEW OF CLAIMING HER BEASTS: BOOK THREE?

You can find it available on amazon.

Please don't forget to leave a review if you enjoyed this work!

Thank you for reading!

www.ingramcontent.com/pod-product-compliance
Lightning Source LLC
Chambersburg PA
CBHW031017190726
48286CB00003BA/895